•••

*Your
Second Life
Begins
When You Realize
You Only
Have One*

•••

Your Second Life Begins When You Realize You Only Have One

RAPHAËLLE GIORDANO

Translated from the French
by Nick Caistor

G. P. Putnam's Sons
New York

PUTNAM
— EST. 1838 —

G. P. PUTNAM'S SONS
Publishers Since 1838
An imprint of Penguin Random House LLC
penguinrandomhouse.com

English translation copyright © 2018 by Nick Caistor
Published in the United States in 2018 by G. P. Putnam's Sons
First published in France in 2015 as *Ta deuxième vie commence quand tu comprends que tu n'en as qu'une* by Groupe Eyrolles copyright © 2015 by Groupe Eyrolles

Library of Congress Cataloging-in-Publication Data

Names: Giordano, Raphaëlle, 1974- author. | Caistor, Nick, translator.
Title: Your second life begins when you realize you only have one /
    Raphaëlle Giordano ; translated from the French by Nick Caistor.
Other titles: Ta deuxiáeme vie commence quand tu comprends
    que tu n'en as qu'une. English
Description: New York : G.P. Putnam's Sons, [2018]
Identifiers: LCCN 2018015685| ISBN 9780525535591 (paperback) |
    ISBN 9780525535614 (epub)
Subjects: LCSH: Self-realization in women—Fiction. | Conduct of life—Fiction. |
    BISAC: FICTION / Contemporary Women. | FICTION / Family Life. |
    FICTION / Literary.
Classification: LCC PQ2707.I68 T313 2018 | DDC 843/.92—dc23
LC record available at https://lccn.loc.gov/2018015685
p.   cm.

Printed in the United States of America
20   19   18   17   16   15   14   13   12

Book design by Ashley Tucker

My dream is that everyone should take
full advantage of their talents
and responsibility for their happiness.
Because there is nothing more important
than to live life to the limits
of one's childhood dreams . . .
Have a good journey.

RAPHAËLLE

Your
Second Life
Begins
When You Realize
You Only
Have One

... one ...

The raindrops crashing against my windshield grew larger and larger. The wipers creaked and shuddered and soon the torrents of water were so great that I instinctively took my foot off the accelerator. It was an almost biblical storm; a car accident was the last thing I needed.

To avoid the Friday-evening traffic on my way back into central Paris, I had decided to take the back roads through the woods that surround the city. Anything to avoid the gridlocked highways and the horror of spending hours at a standstill. I squinted as I tried to make out the road signs ahead through the misted-up windows. And as if the weather and the traffic weren't enough, all of a sudden, in the middle of the dark wood, my GPS gave up the ghost.

It has to be said, no GPS would ever have survived the journey I'd just made. Or at least not unscathed. I was returning from an uncharted wilderness, the sort of area where "you are here" means "you are nowhere." And yet . . . out there was a small office park, an unlikely collection of PLCs (*Profitless companies,* I thought to myself) that my boss must have thought offered enough of a commercial opportunity to justify my trip. Although I had the unpleasant suspicion that ever since he'd agreed I could work a four-day week, he was making me pay for that favor by giving me the jobs no one else wanted. Which explained why I was in this tin can on wheels, navigating the roads on the outskirts of Paris to chase after such small fry . . .

Come on, Camille, stop feeling sorry for yourself and concentrate on the road . . .

Suddenly there was a loud bang. I swerved terrifyingly out of control. My head hit the windshield, and I learned that the story about your life flashing in front of your eyes in a split second wasn't just a myth.

After a few foggy moments, I came to and tentatively reached up to where I'd hit my forehead . . . nothing sticky, thank goodness, just a large bump. I quickly checked myself all over. No, no other injuries to report. More of a fright than anything else, thank god!

I got out of the car, shielding myself from the rain as best I could with my raincoat, and went to inspect the damage: a burst tire and a dented fender. Once I got over my initial panic, fear gave way to anger. *For fuck's sake!* Could today possibly get any worse? With shaking hands, I grabbed my cell phone as if it was a lifeline. No signal, of course. Why was I not surprised?

The minutes ticked by. Nothing—there wasn't a soul around. I was all alone, stranded in this empty wood.

Don't just panic, do something! There must *be people living round here somewhere . . .*

So I abandoned the car—it was no use to me now—and set off along the road, braving the elements in my oh-so-glamorous hi-vis waterproof. Needs must . . .

After an eternity of ten minutes, I came across the iron gates of a large house. I pressed the button on the videophone as urgently as if I were dialing emergency services.

A man replied tersely, in one of those haughty voices that you reserve for unwanted callers.

"Yes? What is it?"

I crossed my fingers: *Please let this guy take pity on me!*

"Good evening . . . So sorry to bother you, but I've crashed my car in the woods behind your house . . . My tire's burst and I don't have any cell recep—"

The buzzing sound of the gate being opened made me jump. Was it my bedraggled shipwreck survivor's appearance that had convinced him to offer me asylum? I didn't care. I slipped inside without a second thought and found myself confronted by a magnificent mansion, surrounded by a manicured garden. I felt as though I had struck gold.

... two ...

The light came on at the top of the front steps, and the door opened. A man's imposing silhouette advanced toward me, carrying an enormous umbrella. When he drew closer, I could make out a long face, good-looking despite the wrinkles. He was one of those men who had aged well: a kind of Gallic Sean Connery. I noticed dimples at the corners of his mouth, which gave him a friendly air. One that put me at ease. He was at least sixty, but it didn't look as if it had taken much effort to get there. His pale gray eyes had a lively twinkle to them, and his salt-and-pepper hair was surprisingly thick for a man his age, only slightly receding in a way that suited the shape of his forehead. A beard as well tended as the gardens finished off his stylish appearance. He invited me to follow him inside.

"Come in. You're soaked through!"

"Tha-thanks. It's really kind of you. Again, I'm so sorry to disturb you . . ."

"Don't be. It's not a problem. Take a seat while I fetch you a towel."

Just then, an elegant woman who I guessed must be his wife appeared. Her pretty face was creased with a frown, which she quickly suppressed when she saw me.

"Is everything all right, darling?"

"Yes, everything's fine. This lady had a car accident and couldn't get a signal in the woods. She just needs to use the phone and to recover a little."

"Oh yes, of course . . ."

When she saw how cold I was, she kindly offered me a cup of tea. I accepted on the spot.

As she disappeared into the kitchen, her husband came back downstairs, holding a towel.

"Thank you, you're very kind, Mr. . . ."

"Call me Claude."

"Ah, OK. My name's Camille."

"Here you are, Camille. The phone is over there."

"Wonderful. I won't be a minute."

"Take your time."

I went over to the telephone, which stood on a pretty inlaid wooden table beneath a piece of modern art. These people had taste, and they were obviously well-off. What a relief I had come across them and not some monster who devoured desperate housewives in distress.

I picked up the receiver and dialed my insurance company's

roadside assistance number. Since I couldn't give them my car's exact location, I asked the mechanic to come to the house, after Claude gave me the address. I was told they would be there within the hour. I breathed a sigh of relief: things were looking up.

Then I called home. Claude was considerate enough to go over to the fire crackling in the hearth on the far side of the room and poke the logs while I did so. After eight seemingly endless rings, my husband picked up. I could tell from his voice that he had fallen asleep in front of the TV. He didn't seem surprised or worried that I was calling: he was used to me sometimes coming home quite late.

I explained all the catastrophes that had occurred, but he kept interrupting me with annoyed grunts and tuts of exasperation, before asking technical details: How long would it take the tow truck to come? How much was it going to cost? My nerves were frayed enough as it was, and the way he was behaving made me want to shout down the phone. Couldn't he show a bit of understanding just this once? After telling him that I would sort it out and he needn't bother to wait up for me, I slammed down the phone.

Despite myself, my hands were trembling and I knew tears were welling in my eyes. I didn't hear Claude coming back over to me, so I jumped when I felt his hand on my shoulder.

"Everything OK? Are you all right?" he asked gently. I only wished my husband's voice on the phone a few moments earlier had sounded as concerned.

He bent over me and said again, "Are you OK?"

At that, something in his face brought my defenses crashing down: my lip began to wobble, and I couldn't hold back the tears. My mascara ran down my face as I released all the pent-up frustration that had built over the previous hours, weeks— months, even . . .

... *three* ...

At first Claude said nothing. He simply stood there, one warm hand resting on my shoulder.

When my tears finally dried, his wife, who in the meantime had put down a steaming cup of tea beside me, went to fetch some tissues. Then she vanished upstairs, no doubt sensing that her presence might inhibit what would be a welcome opportunity to get things off my chest.

"I'm . . . I'm so sorry, this is ridiculous. I don't know what's come over me. I've been on edge recently anyway, and I've had such a terrible day—it's all too much."

Claude had gone to sit in the armchair opposite me and was listening closely. Something about him made me feel I could trust him. He looked me straight in the eye. It was not a judgmental, intrusive look—more like a pair of open arms.

Gazing at him, I sensed that I could open up. My inner resistance crumbled. So much the worse. Or so much the better?

I told him the main reasons why I felt so down. I explained

how all the micro-frustrations had accumulated and eaten away at any enthusiasm I felt for life, just when it seemed I should have everything I needed to feel on top of the world.

"It's not that I'm unhappy, but I'm not especially happy either . . . It's so awful, this feeling that joy has slipped through my fingers. I don't want to see a doctor about it: he would probably tell me I was depressed and stuff me full of drugs. No, it's just this sort of . . . dissatisfaction. It's nothing serious, but . . . it's as if my heart simply isn't in it anymore. I'm sorry, I really don't know if any of this is making sense."

What I said seemed to move him so much that I wondered if it hadn't struck a very personal chord. Although we had only met barely an hour before, a strange feeling of trust had sprung up between us. My confession had suddenly brought us several degrees closer and established a surprising bond.

He obviously felt a genuine desire to comfort me.

"Well, you may know what Abbé Pierre said: 'We have as much need of reasons for living as of the necessities of life.' So don't say it's not serious. It's tremendously serious! Troubles of the soul are not something to be taken lightly. And listening to you, I actually think I know what's wrong."

"You do? Really?" I sniffled.

"Yes . . ."

He hesitated a moment before continuing, as if trying to work out whether I was going to be receptive to what he had to say. He must have decided I was, because he went on, as though revealing a great secret.

"You're probably suffering from a kind of acute routinitis."

"A-what?"

"Acute routinitis. It's a sickness of the soul that affects more and more people in the world, especially in the West. The symptoms are almost always the same: a lack of motivation; chronic dissatisfaction; feeling you've lost your bearings and everything meaningful in life; finding it hard to feel happy even though you have more than enough material goods; disenchantment; world-weariness . . ."

"But . . . but how do you know all that?"

"I'm a routinologist."

"A routine-what?"

He must be used to this kind of reaction, because he remained calm and collected while still projecting compassion.

He briefly explained what routinology was: an innovative method still little known in France but already popular in many other parts of the world. Researchers and scientists had come to realize that an increasing number of people were suffering from the syndrome. While not being clinically depressed, one could still have a feeling of emptiness and unease and suffer from the unpleasant sensation that although you had everything you needed to be happy, you didn't have the key to make the most of it.

I listened to him wide-eyed, drinking in what he was saying. It was such an accurate description of what I was feeling. My expression encouraged him to continue.

"You know, at first glance routinitis may seem like a benign condition, but it can cause real damage: epidemics of pessimism, tsunamis of discontent, catastrophic storms of bad moods. Smiling could become endangered. Don't laugh, it's true! Not to mention the butterfly effect. The more the phenomenon spreads, the greater number of people fall prey to it . . . If not properly treated, routinitis can lower the well-being index of an entire country."

Although I knew he was being serious, I also realized he was laying it on thick to bring a smile back to my face.

"Isn't that a bit of an exaggeration?"

"Only slightly. You can't imagine how many happiness illiterates there are. Not to mention all those lacking any emotional intelligence. It's a real scourge. Don't you agree that there's nothing worse than the sense that life is passing you by? Simply because you don't have the courage to go for what you really want, because you haven't stayed faithful to your deepest-seated values, to the dreams you harbored as a child?"

"Yes, that's so true . . ."

"Unfortunately, developing our capacity for being happy isn't something we're taught at school. Yet there are techniques you can learn. You can have lots of money and be really unhappy, or equally not have much but make your existence the sweetest there is. The capacity for being happy has to be worked on, built up day by day. All you have to do is take a good look at your system of values and re-educate the way you look at life and what's going on around you."

He stood up and went over to the big table to fetch a plate of cookies to go with my tea. He nibbled a few absentmindedly, seemingly keen to return to our conversation. The more I listened to him telling me about how important it was to rediscover yourself, to love yourself better so as to find your own path and your happiness, to make that joy radiate around you, the more I wondered what on earth could have happened to him to make him so passionate about all this.

He lit up completely as he tried to persuade me to share his conviction. Then all at once he fell silent and stared at me with that benevolent look of his that seemed to read my mind as easily as a blind person reading Braille.

"You know, Camille, most things that happen to you depend on what goes on up here," he said, tapping his skull. "In your head. The things that happen in the mind are full of surprises. You can't imagine just how far your thoughts influence your reality . . . Like Plato's description in his Allegory of the Cave: chained up in a cave, mankind creates a false image of reality, because all he knows of it are the flickering images of the things that a fire lit behind him throws onto the wall in front."

I couldn't help seeing the funny side of the situation, although I said nothing. I had to admit, I hadn't expected a philosophy lecture in such cozy surroundings only an hour after a car accident.

"You're comparing Plato's allegory to the way our minds function? Wow . . ."

He smiled at my reaction.

"Of course; I think there's a similarity with those thoughts that put a screen between reality and ourselves, distorting it with beliefs, presumptions, and prejudices . . . and who is doing all that? Your mind. Nothing but your mind! I call it the 'thoughts factory.' It's a real assembly line. The good news is that you have the power to change those thoughts. It's up to you whether you see the glass as half empty or half full. You can work on your mind-set so that it stops playing tricks on you. All you need is the method, a little patience, and perseverance."

I was stunned. I didn't know whether he was raving mad or if I should wholeheartedly applaud his incredible pep talk. In the end I did neither, simply nodding in agreement.

He must have sensed that for the moment he had reached the limit of the information I could digest.

"I'm sorry. Do you find my theories annoying?"

"No, not at all. They sound really interesting. It's just that I'm a bit tired. Don't take any notice of me."

"Of course, that's only natural. If you like, I could talk to you again about this method another time . . . It's really been proved to help people recover a sense of purpose and rebuild a fulfilling life for themselves."

He stood up and went over to a pretty little cherrywood writing desk. He took out a business card and handed it to me.

"Come and see me whenever you like," he said, smiling softly.

I read:

Claude DUPONTEL
Routinologist
15, rue de la Boétie
75008 Paris

The card also had his cell and landline. I took it from him without really knowing what to make of all this yet. To be polite, I told him I'd think about it. This didn't seem to faze him, and he didn't insist. As a salesperson, that surprised me: Didn't anyone who was self-employed jump at the chance to secure a new client? The fact that he was not at all pushy seemed to me to indicate a rare self-confidence. It made me feel that if I turned down his offer, I would be the one losing out.

But at that moment, I was still feeling the effect of everything that had happened that evening: the stupid accident, the stupid storm like something out of a bad horror movie . . . And on top of it all: a routinologist. I thought I'd started imagining things. In the next five minutes, the camera crew would appear and someone would shout, "Gotcha!"

The doorbell rang. But it wasn't a cameraman or a TV presenter: just the tow-truck guy.

"Would you like us to come with you?" Claude asked.

"No, thanks so much. I'll be fine. You've already been very kind. I don't know how to thank you . . ."

"It was nothing. Anyone would have done the same. Send us a text when you get home."

"I will. Good-bye, and thanks again."

I climbed up into the cab with the mechanic to show him the way, taking a last look back through the truck window. I saw Claude and his wife standing on the steps arm in arm, waving a brief good-bye. They seemed such a loving, sharing couple.

With this image of peaceful happiness etched into my mind, we bumped off into the darkness, back to reality . . .

... *four* ...

I woke up the next morning with a terrible migraine that lasted all day. I had spent the night tossing and turning, thinking over everything Claude Dupontel had told me. Was I really a victim of acute routinitis? Did the anxiety that had held me in its grip for several weeks now really mean I had to embark on a course of counseling? What, in fact, did I really have to complain about? I had a husband and a son and a job that offered me security. Maybe I just needed to pull myself together and stop wallowing. And yet my thirty-something middle-class discontent wouldn't let me go. I had tried often enough to sweep it under the carpet, without success.

I did occasionally try to put things into perspective. To "see the bigger picture," as they say in women's magazines. I ran through the whole gamut of human misery in my mind. People in war zones. People with serious illnesses. The homeless, jobless, loveless . . . Compared to them, my problems seemed so petty. But as Claude Dupontel had said, there was no point comparing what couldn't be compared. The scale of happiness or misery isn't the same for everyone. I didn't know him, and yet he seemed so well-adjusted, so centered. Yes, "centered" was the word. Of course, I didn't believe in miracle cures that transform your life with the wave of a magic wand. But he seemed so convincing when he said that things really could change. He insisted that feeling down and stuck in a rut was not inevitable, that you can choose to be someone who does not allow daily existence to grind her down, but who lives life to the full. To turn your life into a work of art . . . It was a project that seemed pretty unrealistic at first, but why not at least try to aim toward it?

In theory, I was all for it. But in practice? "One day I'll go to live in Theory, because in Theory everything is wonderful . . ." So, how to get started, to get beyond the stage of shoulda coulda woulda? With all this playing on my mind, I struggled out of bed. I felt as though I'd been beaten black and blue during the night. To top it all off, without meaning to, I put my left foot on the floor first. I know it's a silly superstition, but I immediately saw this as a bad omen: the instinctive reaction of a brain swamped with negative vibes. The day was off to a bad start.

Sebastien, my alleged nearest and dearest, hardly even bothered to say good morning. He wrestled with a disobedient tie, and in between his stifled swearing I thought I made out that he was late for a meeting. So he wasn't going to be taking Adrien to school today, either. Sigh.

Adrien, my son, is nine years, six months, ten days, and eight hours old, as he would be only too happy to inform you. I found his rush to grow up both touching and slightly terrifying; it was all moving so quickly. Too quickly. Adrien had always done everything faster than usual. The only way to have stopped him would have been to tie him to a chair. We soon had to get used to the idea that our son was an "Energizer bunny": he never wore out.

But I did. Even though I loved him more than anything in the world, there were days when I thought he must have a mini energy-sucking vacuum cleaner under his T-shirt.

Of course, we were modern parents—we'd practically been weaned on the belief that the child is a fully-fledged individual with a right to be heard. But experience had taught us that our way of bringing him up had been far too liberal. By sticking to the ideals of dialogue and respect for a child's personality, we had given our son far too much freedom.

"Boundaries!" my mother never stopped yelling at me.

She was right, of course.

Boundaries: that was what I had been trying to establish for several months now, in an attempt to correct our overlax attitude. I had done a U-turn and gone from one extreme to the other. No doubt I was now being too tough on him . . . but you just do your best, don't you? I was constantly whining at Adrien in an effort to keep him in line. He would whine back but comply in the end. In spite of his rebellious side, deep down he was a good kid.

I knew I was on his back a lot—for his own good, I was sure, although at times I felt I was turning into a real nag. I hated being like that. "Tidy your room, take a shower, switch the lights off, do your homework, put the toilet seat down . . ." I had exchanged my "good" mom approach for the "bad" mom one. And everything I had gained in neatly folded socks had been lost in terms of my relationship with him. There was a tug-of-war going on between us. We were cat and dog, as if we no longer understood each other. Then again, how could he act like such a teenager when he wasn't even ten yet?

All this was going through my head when I walked into his room. We had to leave the house in ten minutes, and he was playing ping-pong against the wall, only half dressed. He had put on odd socks, hadn't bothered to comb his hair, and his bedroom looked as though a bomb had gone off in it—not that he had noticed.

He looked at me with his chestnut-brown eyes and their astonishingly long lashes, as enchanting as ever. I paused for a moment to consider his round face and strong features, his well-defined mouth, which was now stuck in a stubborn pout. Even when it was this untidy, his hair was so lovely and soft it made you want to stroke it. He was a gorgeous little devil. I resisted the temptation to go and hug him and smooth it down, the rascal. I was the drill sergeant, determined to make sure he was in step.

"But, Mommmmm! What's your problem? Stay cool. Chill out," he replied, underlining his words with a Zen rapper hand gesture he'd learned from the latest YouTube clip.

That drove me crazy. I yelled at him and then slammed into the bathroom for a shower. I washed hastily, already dreading what was on the day's to-do list.

As I stepped out of the shower, my reflection in the mirror only made me frown more. A deep furrow was plowed across my forehead.

I stared at this face that used to be pretty—and maybe still could be, if my skin weren't so sallow and the bags under the green eyes that had once been so seductive weren't so dark. Just as could my blond silky hair, when I found the time to style it properly to frame my round face. A little too round these days, due to the weight I had put on after my pregnancy and the sweet treats I had given in to in the years since then. Annoyed, I grabbed the lifeline of mother's little helpers and swallowed far too quickly, considering their expiration date. By now I was in a thoroughly bad mood.

As I rushed back into the bedroom to get dressed, I carelessly knocked over the photo frame on the bedside table. I picked it up to put it back. It was a great photo of me and Sebastien at a time when we would stargaze and laugh all night long . . . What had happened to that handsome man with flashing eyes who knew just what to whisper in my ear to make me go weak at the knees? How long had it been since he had made the slightest attempt to seduce me? And yet, he was a good, kind man. Really kind. Thinking about the tenderness that had slowly and subtly replaced the passion of our early days, I felt vaguely sick . . . Over the years the once wild, lush jungle of our love for each other had been transformed into a formal French garden: everything neat and tidy, with not a single blade of grass out of place.

Shouldn't love spill out, burst into flame, boil over, erupt uncontrollably?

Anyway, that was how things were now. What had been the tipping point? When Adrien had come on the scene? When Sebastien had been promoted? Who knew? Whatever the reason, the outcome was the same. Stuck in this marital mud, hemmed in by an existence that ran along too smoothly, I realized that our life as a couple had, like a piece of chewing gum you've chewed for too long, lost all its flavor.

Chasing away these unpleasant thoughts with a wave of the hand, I threw on the first thing I could find. Who cared about grace or elegance? Who would they be for, and why? Ever since I'd entered into a partnership for life, I was no longer of interest to anyone. Might as well be comfortable.

I dropped off my son at school, nagging him all the way to hurry. Hurrying was the huge bugbear of all our lives. It laid down the law, punished us like an all-powerful tyrant, and made us submit to the crushing power of the hands on the clock face. You had only to look at those people ready to crush others in order to cram onto an already packed Métro car because they can't bear to wait for the next train in three minutes, or who run a red light to save a few seconds at the risk of a serious accident, or talk on the phone while they are tapping away at a computer and eating at the same time . . .

I was no different. Since I had no car after the accident, I ran to the Métro and almost went flying down the stairs.

Great idea, Camille. Break a leg just so you don't miss your train.

Out of breath, sweating freely despite the cold, I collapsed onto a seat, wondering how on earth I was going to get through the day ahead of me.

... *five* ...

When I left Claude Dupontel's house a week earlier, I had
slipped his card into my coat pocket. Every day since then I
had felt it, turning it over and over, without ever making up my
mind to call him. It was only on the ninth day, as I was coming
out of a heated meeting where my boss had told me off in front
of everyone, that I decided this couldn't go on: things had to
change. I didn't really know how or where to start, but I suspected that if anyone did, it would be Claude.

I called him during my lunch break. My stomach was still
churning from that morning's meeting.

The phone rang several times before he picked up.

"Mr. Dupontel?"

"Speaking."

"It's Camille . . . Do you remember me?"

"Of course. Good morning, Camille. How are you?"

"Good, thank you. Well, actually, not all that good. That's
why I'm calling."

"Oh yes?"

"You offered to tell me a bit more about your happiness method. I'm really interested in it, so if you're free . . ."

"Let's see. Would this Friday at seven p.m. be any good?"

I quickly wondered what I could do about Adrien and decided that he could stay home alone for a while, just until his father got back from work.

"OK, I can manage that. Thanks so much. I'll see you on Friday then."

"See you on Friday, Camille. Take care."

Take care. The words were still echoing in my mind as I walked back to the office. It was so nice to have someone be concerned about me. An ounce of kindness in a world of selfish boors—a world I knew very well, as I was the only woman in a team of eight salespeople. The insults flew round the office all day, schoolboy humor that was often cruel. I found it exhausting. I really wanted something different. For relationships to be more honest, perhaps. Of course, I was very pleased to have a job at all. Nowadays having a permanent position was a luxury, as my mother never ceased telling me.

Ah, my mother. My father had left her soon after I was born, and even if he hadn't completely vanished—he occasionally sent her money—she had struggled to get by as a single mother and had always given me the impression she was hard up. So when the moment came for me to choose a career, there was no option except to go down whatever path she thought would be the most profitable. Something that would be lucrative, so that I would be financially independent whatever happened. I had always been passionate about drawing, but I had to put aside my creative ideas and force myself to enroll in a business studies course. I had found my career path—on the surface, at least—but inside me, something wasn't right. Consigning your childhood dream to the garbage is a sure way to put your heart out of joint.

The day I graduated was without doubt the happiest day of my mother's life, apart from when I was born. I was going to have a brighter future than hers. Her joy was a balm for my misgivings, so that in the end I persuaded myself that things weren't so bad. My career started very well: I was good with other people. Then my marriage and Adrien's birth put a brake on my ambitions. I decided to go part-time to be able to enjoy my son. I naïvely thought this was the best solution, without realizing all the drawbacks: apart from having to do in four days what others did in five, I got the distinct impression that I had fallen in the estimation of my colleagues and superiors. I was devalued in a way I thought was unfair.

My permanent job had coincided with a permanent relationship. Twelve years' plain sailing—with a few ups and downs, of course, but no great storms. On the verge of turning forty—thirty-eight and a quarter, to be precise (my god, why do those grains of sand seem to slip faster and faster through the hourglass?)—I had achieved a reasonable amount: a husband who had stayed with me (I had apparently escaped the family curse of the abandoned wife, but I occasionally felt it was hanging over me like the sword of Damocles); a wonderful child (wasn't his boister-ousness simply a sign of how he was thriving?); and a job that more than fulfilled its purpose in terms of financial rewards, with the added bonus from time to time of enabling me to secure a client of my own.

So everything was more or less all right. More or less. And it was precisely this "more or less" that made me so keen to go and see Claude Dupontel. A simple "more or less" that concealed some big "why"s and brought with it a whole series of reassessments. As I was about to discover.

On the day of our appointment, I found myself outside an elegant nineteenth-century stone building with cast-iron balconies and decorated moldings. A caryatid seemed to look askance at me as I went in through a big doorway and reached a luxurious vestibule. I was so intimidated I almost crept into the interior courtyard, which was beautifully paved and filled with a whole range of stylish greenery. A haven in the urban jungle. "The first door on the left at the far end of the courtyard," Claude Dupontel had told me.

No sooner had I rung the bell than a small, slender woman opened the door, as if she had been behind it, waiting for me.

"Are you Camille?" she asked directly, with a broad smile.

"Er, yes, that's me," I replied, slightly taken aback.

She asked me to follow her down a long corridor. I had the impression she was shooting curious, amused glances at me. As we passed a mirror, I couldn't help checking to make sure my lipstick wasn't smudged and that there was nothing odd about what I was wearing. I couldn't see anything wrong.

She left me in a waiting room filled with soft, deep chairs, telling me that Mr. Dupontel would see me in a moment. I became absorbed in the modern art decorating the walls, enjoying the intertwined shapes and subtle play of colors. The assistant reappeared a few minutes later, with another client. A young woman who I guessed could be no more than thirty sat in an armchair on my left. A stylish brunette. I envied her svelte figure and chic appearance. Catching me looking at her, she smiled.

"Do you have an appointment with Claude?"

"Yes."

"Is this your first time?"

"Yes."

"You'll see, he's extraordinary. He's worked miracles with me. Of course, his method is a little surprising at first, but then . . ."

She leaned over toward me, obviously intending to go on, but at that moment the door opened and Claude Dupontel appeared.

"Ah, Sophie, there you are. Good evening, Camille. We'll only be a second. We just have to deal with something briefly and then I'll be with you."

The young woman called Sophie jumped up as though Claude were someone she would follow to the ends of the earth. I heard her laughter tinkle along the corridor: they seemed to get on like a house on fire. The door to his office closed behind them. It opened again shortly afterward, and once again I heard her tinkling laugh. Now it was my turn.

I stealthily wiped my hand on my coat, hoping to get rid of the telltale traces of moisture. How stupid to get nervous because I was visiting him like this—I was only curious.

"Camille? Come with me, it's along here . . ."

I followed him into his office, which was again surprisingly elegant.

"Please, take a seat. I'm delighted to see you," he said with a smile that matched his words. "If you're here, it must be because you want to change certain things in your life. Is that right?"

"Yes. At least, I think so . . . What you told me the other day really intrigued me, and I'd like to know more."

"Briefly, I need to warn you that it's not a conventional counseling method, in the sense that it takes more of a practical approach than a theoretical one. We start from the principle that it's not within these walls that anyone who wishes to change will discover the truth or understand the meaning of her life. No, it's only through action, through actual experience. Apart from that, the method draws on the teachings of several schools of philosophical, spiritual, and even scientific thought. It adopts the most tried-and-tested personal-development techniques from all round the world. It's a summary of what mankind has found most useful in order to evolve positively."

"OK, I get it. 'Understanding the meaning of life.' That

resonates with me, of course, but isn't that what we all want? It's like the Holy Grail. But it's incredibly hard to find, and I've no idea where to start looking."

"Don't worry. 'Giving your life meaning' is the common thread of all change. In practice, you advance stage by stage."

"Stage by stage?"

"Yes. It's obvious that you don't become a black belt of change overnight. That's why I apply the 'theory of small steps' to help my clients progress gradually. When we talk of change, lots of people imagine something huge and radical, but decisive life changes start with small, apparently insignificant transformations. It may be that sometimes my advice sounds self-evident, almost too obvious. But make no mistake: it's not managing to do things once that's complicated; it's doing them every day. 'We are what we repeat over and over,' according to Aristotle. That's so true. To become a better, happier, more balanced person calls for regular work and effort. You'll find that the difficulty isn't knowing what you ought to be doing to feel better, but to commit yourself completely and to move from theory to practice."

"And what makes you believe I'm capable of it at all?"

"I'm not the one who has to believe it—you do. But rather than asking yourself if you're capable of being happier, start by asking yourself if you really want it. Do you, Camille?"

"Er, yes . . . Yes, I think so."

He smiled kindly, then asked me to come and look at the clippings pinned to the wall near his desk. I joined him.

There were photographs of happy people, apparently enjoying whatever it was they most wanted to do; postcards sent from far-flung, exotic locations; all kinds of thank-you notes.

"Just like you, all these people had their doubts at the outset. It's only normal, to begin with. What you need is to really *want* to take the leap. Do you feel motivated to change, Camille?"

I tried to delve into my innermost feelings.

"Yes, yes I do. Even if it scares me a little, I really want things to change. But how? That's what I'm not clear about."

"That's typical. To help you have a better idea, are you willing to carry out a little exercise that doesn't commit you to anything and will only take a few minutes?"

"Yes, why not?"

"Good. Then I'd like you to write down everything you'd like to change in your life. And I mean everything, from the most trivial to the most essential. Is that OK?"

"Yes, of course."

He sat me down at a small writing desk in a corner of the room, where sheets of paper and pens of all kinds were waiting for the candidates-for-a-better-life.

"I'll leave you to it. I'll be back in a minute," he said, smiling encouragement.

I found this a fairly simple exercise. I spooled through the film of my life and began to note down anything that occurred to me. I was pleased to see how easily the ideas flowed but rather less happy to realize how long my list was becoming. As I wrote,

I became aware of all the frustrations that had been building up, and it came as a shock.

When Claude Dupontel reappeared, he had the good grace not to raise his eyebrows at the length of my list. All he said was, "That's very good."

I couldn't help but feel that little stab of joy that schoolgirls get when they are praised by their teacher.

But then I thought, *That's nonsense! There's really no reason to be so happy that you've got such a long list of frustrations.*

He must have read my mind, because he said, to reassure me, "You can be proud of yourself. It's very hard to be brave enough to put down on paper everything that seems wrong with your life. You should congratulate yourself."

"I have difficulty being proud of myself in general . . ."

"That's something that can soon be changed."

"From where I sit, that's hard to believe."

"Yet it's the very first thing I'm going to ask of you, Camille: to believe that. Are you ready for it?"

"Oh . . . Yes . . . I think so. Well, I mean, yes, I'm sure!"

"That's the spirit! 'Change is a door that can only be opened from the inside,' as the saying goes. Which means, Camille, that you are the only one who can decide to change. I can help you. But I need you to be totally committed."

"What do you mean by 'totally committed'?" I asked, vaguely disturbed.

"Simply that you become completely involved in the process. Don't worry: nothing I propose will ever be dangerous or more than you can manage. We'll work together within an ethical framework that respects how you are progressing. The only objective is to help you make those positive breakthroughs that will lead to change."

"What if at some point I decide I don't like the method?"

"You're under no obligation to continue. If you want to stop, you can. But if you decide to continue, I'll ask you to commit yourself four hundred percent. That's how the best results are achieved."

"How long does this kind of counseling last, as a rule?"

"However long it takes someone to refashion his or her life project so that it brings happiness."

"Hmm. I see . . . One last question. You haven't said how much all this costs, and I don't know if I'm going to be able to afford it . . ."

"As far as money goes, routinology operates in a very special, even unique manner, but one that's been proved to work. You will only pay me what you think you owe me, and then only when you have succeeded. If my method fails and you're not satisfied, you won't have to pay a thing."

"What? But that's completely crazy! How do you make a living like that? And how can you be sure that people will be honest enough to pay you someday?"

"That's the way you see the world at the moment, Camille. But I can assure you that because I have faith in things like trust, shared knowledge, and unconditional support, the people I've helped have been more than generous once they have achieved their goals. I believe in every person's potential to succeed, as long as they show respect for their own nature and most cherished values. All you have to do is make your life project properly fit in with who you are. That demands a real commitment and a lot of effort. You will have to be methodical about it—but it's worth it!"

"Have you ever failed?"

"Never . . . Right, we can stop here for today. I'll let you think all this over at your leisure. One option would be for you to embark on the first stage to see what you think of it. If you get results, you carry on. If not, you stop."

"I'll think about it. Thank you, Claude."

He led me back to the door and gave me a firm handshake, that of someone who knows what he wants in life. I envied him.

"I'll let you have my decision very soon. Good-bye, Claude."

"Take your time. Good-bye, Camille."

... *six* ...

Outside in the street once more, I felt like a stranger to myself: the interview had turned my world upside down. My hands were trembling a little, but I didn't know whether it was from fear or excitement. As I walked toward the Métro, thoughts were racing through my brain. With every step I took, I recalled the things that Claude had said, and my determination grew: "Everyone has a duty toward life, don't you think? To learn to know ourselves, to become aware that time is short, to make choices that matter and that mean something. And above all, not to waste our talents . . . We must fulfill our potential, Camille. Urgently!"

That evening, I went over what my life was at present. It was all very comfy: a safe job, a safe love life . . . But that was simply window dressing. It was high time that I took a proper look at what was underneath and assumed responsibility for it.

As a mother, things were tense. Recently, that tension between my son and me had become electric. Everything was a chore. What with his school, his clubs and hobbies and medical appointments, it felt as if I no longer had a minute to myself. As soon as I set foot inside our front door, I felt harassed and my tolerance threshold dropped dramatically. I flew off the handle at next to nothing. Especially over homework, which had tripled that school year thanks to an overzealous teacher. Already tired from school, Adrien saw this workload as punishment. It seemed endless, and I felt I was dragging him along like a dead donkey. I shouted at him; he exploded back at me, either bursting into tears or becoming hysterical.

I was so exhausted by it all that once he had finally completed his work, I would let him do whatever he wanted—and he would rush off to plonk himself in front of a screen. I knew that this was the easy way out, but I needed a bit of peace, to unwind for five minutes. *It's only human, isn't it?* I would reassure myself.

Often, he would want me to come and look at the imaginary world he had created on Minecraft, his favorite computer game of the moment, or an unmissable YouTube video.

"I don't have the time, sweet pea; I have to get supper ready."

That was how it was. Over the past few months, I hadn't had the energy to take an interest in his world, and without properly realizing it, this had created a gulf between us. He would wander off again, disappointed and vaguely sad.

"You never do anything with me anymore!" he would say reproachfully.

I struggled to justify myself. "Adrien, try to understand. You're a big boy now. The house doesn't run itself! Besides, with all the games you have . . ."

"But I have no one to play them with! Why can't you give me a little brother?"

There he went, making me feel guilty again. Why, as a modern European woman, should I be obliged to have 2.4 children? What if I wanted only one?

Social pressure: that got on my nerves as well. All year round, my ears were filled with the same old refrain: "It's so sad to be an only child. He must get bored . . ."

Sebastien had been disappointed when I confessed I didn't want any more children. Had that also contributed to the distance between us? That and the daily routine. The draining effect of monotony, of the ordinary. We no longer feel obliged to make an effort, so in the end we stop making any effort at all. We just grow careless. It's so obvious, right under our noses, and yet we don't see it.

I had reached this stage in my reflections when I glanced over at my husband. He was stretched out on the sofa, half watching TV while he played on his smartphone. He was oblivious to my presence, and above all to my inner turmoil. That did it. Yes, at that instant I knew that I wanted to stop settling for this nice little existence that had become such a rut it no longer had any meaning. I wanted to have the courage to shake up everything that was so well established, so predictable, so settled. Exchange the reassuring for the exhilarating! In other words, to press the reset button and start all over again.

I tapped out a text message to Claude Dupontel and immediately pressed Send, like someone drawing up a ladder behind her to make sure there is no going back. If I thought any more about all this, there was a risk that I might back out.

I've made my mind up to give your method a try. I've nothing to lose, have I?

Half an hour later, I jumped when I heard my mobile ping.

Bravo for taking this first step, Camille. It's always the hardest, but I'm sure you won't regret it. Keep an eye on your mailbox. You'll be receiving my first instructions by post. Take care, Claude.

I was pleased. Excited. Nervous. All three at once.

I spent a restless night dreaming I was heading down a ski slope at breakneck speed. I was elated until I suddenly realized that however hard I tried, there was no way I could stop . . . I woke up covered in sweat and paralyzed with fear.

I was so anxious to get home and open my letter box that the workday seemed endless.

What a disappointment! It was empty.

Don't be so impatient! You're hardly his first priority.

Next day, the box was empty again. Another disappointment.

It's not even been forty-eight hours.

The day after . . . empty!

I was champing at the bit. My excitement had turned to frustration. When was I going to start, for heaven's sake? After eight days of feverish waiting, I gave in and telephoned Claude. His assistant answered with that dreamy voice of hers, seemingly designed to calm all expressions of impatience.

"I'm sorry, Mr. Dupontel is in meetings all day. May I give him a message?"

"Oh, yes, thanks. I'd like to know when my course is to start."

"What did he say the last time you saw him?"

"To await his instructions, which I'd receive by post."

"If that's what he said, then you only have to wait. Goodbye. Have a good day."

This time, her mellifluous voice really wound me up. I hung up, furious, in such a state that I was ready to tear up the first thing I could lay my hands on.

... *seven* ...

Three days later, I finally received the letter I had been so eagerly awaiting. I'd been patient for eleven days. I felt the slightly lumpy envelope, trying desperately to guess what it contained.

Inside I found a chain that I immediately recognized as a charm necklace. An adorable little white lotus pendant was attached to it.

I quickly unfolded the short letter from Claude:

Hello, Camille,

I'm so pleased you've decided to take this first step toward reconquering your life! I have total confidence in you and wish you the best of luck in reaching your goals. To welcome and encourage you, I'm giving you this first charm: a white lotus. Each time you've made decisive progress, reached a "level of change," you will receive a new lotus charm, in a different color. As in martial arts, the color code depends on the level you have reached: white for a beginner, then yellow, green, purple . . . up to the black lotus, which means you have reached the final stage of change. That will signify you have attained all your objectives.

Delighted with the idea, I twisted the pendant between my fingers, then read on:

These past few days, without you realizing it, your initiation has already started and has taught you the first lesson: never simply wait for something to happen. You have spent your time watching out for my instructions, for me to tell you what to do. Yet you could already have begun to act on your own behalf. Just remember, Camille: you're the one and only person who can change your life. The impetus has to come from you. I'll be your guide, but I won't *do* anything for you. Write this sentence on a Post-it and look at it every day:

"I am the only one responsible for my life and happiness."

Now here is your first task: you are going to carry out a complete spring-clean, inside and out. By this I mean first an inner cleanup. You must identify everything about you that seems toxic, negative, that hampers your relationships and the way you organize your life. I call it "personal ecology"! At the same time, you need to have an external spring-clean of the things in your home. You are to throw away at least ten useless objects and to tidy up, sort out, and refresh your surroundings in every way possible. Bring me photos of this the next time we meet. You have two weeks to do this. Meanwhile you can of course tell me of any difficulties in an e-mail or text message. I will always make time to answer. Good luck and see you soon!

The letter slipped from my hands. What a list! The idea of turning into Marie Kondo didn't exactly inspire me. And given the state of my house, I had my work cut out . . . Not to mention having no time to do it. I always came back pretty late from work to compensate for working only part-time, and as for Wednesdays, supposedly my free day, they were a real marathon of extracurricular activities and medical appointments for Adrien. Claude had forgotten one small detail: I wasn't a housewife. I didn't have empty days ahead of me.

I immediately shared my concern with him in a text message:

Hello. "Mission Spring-Clean" impossible. Never have time. Suggestions? Yours, Camille.

I anxiously awaited his reply. It arrived in an e-mail later that day:

Dear Camille,

Time as such is not a problem. Only your mind-set makes it one. If you convince yourself that time *is* a problem, it will be. If on the other hand you are convinced that you will succeed in finding time, you'll probably be able to. Try . . . You'll see, your brain believes what you tell it. But don't worry, we will have a proper discussion about mind-sets and positive thinking soon enough. For now, try to see how you can devote a quarter or half an hour to your task in the evening or on the weekend. And remember: energy creates energy. At first, these efforts will seem very difficult, but then less and less so. The more you do, the more you'll want to do!

Good luck.
Claude

So he wanted me to become the Rocky of the feather duster? OK, I'd show him what I was made of.

That same evening, as soon as Adrien was in bed, I armed myself for an all-out assault on dust and disorder. On the way back from the office I had bought armloads of garbage bags and all kinds of cleaning products. Let the battle begin.

Sebastien followed these maneuvers with wide eyes in which I detected a mocking gleam that I took for skepticism. I couldn't care less. Nothing was going to stop my domestic tornado. Well, nothing until I opened the closet in the hallway and saw piles of papers overflowing from battered, split-open boxes; useless bric-a-brac you might have found in the most unlikely flea markets, from a discarded doll to a garden lantern (we don't have a garden); heaps of clothes tottering like a house of cards—clothes that were too small, too big, worn out, holey jumpers, moth-eaten jumpers, pilled jumpers; badminton racquets stuck in an unused fitness step; souvenir tins with the lighter from a long-forgotten concert; unopened letters, letters opened but from people whose faces I could no longer recall, from people I loved but with whom I'd lost touch; a packet of scented handkerchiefs found in a souvenir shop in the first flush of romance; a photo of my first boyfriend (how could I ever possibly have been in love with *him*?); a school notebook; a bag of sugarcoated almond favors from my wedding day that were all stuck together after all these years but that I'd kept for some inexplicable reason . . .

I dragged all of it out of the closet. Faced with this mountain full of dust, I admit I almost threw in the towel. But as I gradually reduced it, I found I was regaining my own space in my head. This "spring-cleaning therapy" was doing me a world of good.

Night after night I gained ground over the disorder. I hunted down the nasty surprises hidden behind pieces of furniture and in the forgotten corners, the objects you did not dare throw away because you had become so used to seeing them. Farewell to rebellious dust, disgusting hairs in the sink, stubborn lime scale, and unsightly rings. I refused to flag or give in and ended up richly rewarded. By the end of the week, the apartment looked almost like a show home. I was over the moon.

"Wow, there's no stopping you, is there?" said Sebastien with feigned irony, in which by now there was a hint of admiration.

"It looks good, doesn't it?" I said.

"Yes, yes, it does. It's just a bit surprising that it's come over you all of a sudden, that's all!"

What? Was I supposed to send him an advance warning? Were there procedural bottlenecks in the art of household happiness, then? His tepid response really pissed me off. I wanted him to share my enthusiasm, to help me. Why did he always behave like a spectator in our married life? I felt like shaking him, telling him how urgent it was for us to change things, that his passivity was not only stifling me but eating away at my feelings for him just as surely as waves eat at a cliff's edge.

THE FOLLOWING WEEKEND, THOUGH, I persuaded my boys to help brighten up our world.

We headed for Home Depot. I was delighted at this final stage, the cherry on the cake of my Mission Spring-Clean. I quickly realized, however, that this was not going to be the jolly outing I had hoped for. We wanted completely different things. Whereas I was dreaming of taking my time in front of every display in search of good ideas, Sebastien wanted to speed through the store at a brisk trot so that he could be out again as quickly as possible. He seemed to think the first can of paint we came across would do the trick. I dragged him round, trying desperately to cast an eye over what was for sale while he sighed and twitched impatiently; my coat hung on my right arm, and Adrien hung on my left. To my horror, my son thought it was hilarious to touch everything we passed. I was almost foaming at the mouth by the time I found the paint department. It was now or never if I wanted to motivate my troops! I was hoping that the evocatively named cans of colors would stir their imagination so that they would finally show a bit of enthusiasm in choosing the one for their bedrooms.

With Adrien, it worked like a charm: he chose the Young Shoots shade, a lawn green that coincided exactly with his passion for soccer. Sebastien was much more hesitant but for the sake of peace and quiet finally accepted an Iced Coffee and a Satin Nougat. I was half satisfied, which was something.

But what happened at the checkout set my nerves so much on edge that I almost dumped everything and left empty-handed. Someone was holding up the line because he wanted to buy some screws and no one knew the price. A hardware assistant was asked to come to the register. I took great pleasure imagining this man having to swallow his screws slowly, one by one. But worse than the delay were all those diabolical last-minute temptations stuck under the noses of children out of their skulls with boredom. What Machiavellian marketing genius dreamed that up? Candy, batteries, flashlights. Naturally,

Adrien wanted something simply for the fun of having it, all the while offering me a brilliant explanation for why he absolutely needed it. I was torn between my increasing irritation and a sense of pride at his convincing spiel.

For the sake of domestic harmony, I gave in and allowed him to buy a packet of apple-flavored Tic Tacs.

"Yes!" he exclaimed, punching the air.

Finally it was our turn. Our bags were filled, then the exit, fresh air, the parking lot, the slamming trunk, Adrien asking us to turn up the volume and singing at the top of his voice. Our silence.

The rest of the weekend was spent in a jumble of drop cloths, rollers, miles of paper towels, old T-shirts covered in paint stains, a pizza party, and improvised camping in the middle of the living room. And afterward, the reward: a brand-new home, and we ourselves, our nostrils saturated with the smell of fresh paint, our arms and legs stiff from having to apply so many coats, happy. Quite simply: happy.

... eight ...

During the week I sent the photos of my home improvements to Claude. He congratulated me, then sent an e-mail explaining what I had to do for the next stage: the inner spring-clean. This was to allow me to identify and get rid of everything polluting my environment and my relationships with others.

"You know, Camille, life is like a hot-air balloon. To go higher we have to know how to lighten the load and to throw overboard all those things that prevent us rising."

As well as this, he asked me to write each aspect of my life that I wanted to see the last of on a separate sheet of paper.

"Bring them all with you on Wednesday at two p.m., if you can, to André Citroën Park in the fifteenth arrondissement. Have a good evening!"

Now what was he up to? Whatever it was, I was sure it would be worth going along with . . . even though at times I wondered where all this was leading me. I felt quite stirred up but sometimes nervous. Wasn't I going to miss my peaceful little existence, which might not involve any big risks but had no great shocks either? No. Definitely not.

I carried on reading his e-mail, which had an attachment and a postscript.

"I'm attaching a very interesting diagram that should help inspire your new mood. It explains the 'vicious circle' and the 'virtuous circle.' Tell me what you think of it."

I clicked on the attachment and discovered two clearly presented columns:

Vicious circle: negative thought > hunched, floppy body position > lack of energy, sadness, discouragement, fears > drifting, apathy, failure to take care of yourself > low self-esteem > "I'm hopeless, I'll never do it" > closing in on yourself, lack of opening up to others > feeling of getting nowhere > lack of vision, uncertain perspectives. Failure, goals not achieved.

Virtuous circle: positive thought or "act as if" > dynamic body position (straight back, head held high, smile) > liveliness, communicative enthusiasm > ability to take care of yourself (eat well, exercise, allow yourself pleasure) > high self-esteem, "I'm worth it, I deserve to be happy" > opening toward others, opportunities, network, ability to bounce back > creativity, constructive view of a situation, solutions. Success, goals achieved.

I thought over this eloquent list. I was beginning to get the general idea and was aware that until now many of my attitudes put me in the vicious-circle column. That just showed how far I still had to go!

I COULD HARDLY WAIT for Wednesday to arrive. I was anxious to find out what Claude had in store for me, and so I walked briskly across the André Citroën Park to reach our meeting place, just below the huge greenhouse. How could I have lived in Paris for so long and not known about this hidden glory of the plant world? As I walked down the avenues, my astonished eyes feasted on the luxuriant vegetation, the beauty of the water features, not to mention the numerous exotic trees and rare species of plants. The walk stirred my senses and reminded me just how absent nature was from my life. I recalled a really interesting article I had read by a Dr. Ian Alcock of the University of Exeter Medical School, published in *Environmental Science & Technology.* In the article, Dr. Alcock studied the relationship over time between mental health and nature (where the satisfaction curve clearly rose from the start and did not stop climbing). His conclusion: nature produced mental improvements on a daily basis for those who lived close to it. What greater encouragement did I need to get out into the country—and go green?

I kept an eye out for Claude and soon saw his tall, angular silhouette, his purposeful walk, his elegant but unfussy clothes. As ever, what struck me most of all was the kind, open expression on his face and the lively eyes that only a person really centered in his existence can have.

We shook hands warmly, and he led me across the gardens. "Where are we going?"

"Over there, can you see?"

"Where, on the lawns?"

"No, just behind them."

I couldn't work out where he meant. All I could see was an enormous tethered hot-air balloon emblazoned with the name Generali. Then all at once I understood.

"You don't mean we're going to . . . ?"

"Yes, we are," he replied, a mischievous glint in his eye. "Have you brought the sheets of paper listing everything you no longer want to keep?"

"Yes. They're all here."

"Good. Show me them."

He read all the sheets of paper carefully.

I no longer want to be too kind.

I no longer want to bend over backward to please other people.

I no longer want to wait passively for things to happen to me.

I no longer want Adrien and me to quarrel all the time.

I no longer want to be ten pounds overweight.

I no longer want to neglect how I look.

I no longer want to let my life as a couple drift along.

I no longer want to feel frustrated by my job.

I no longer want my important decisions to depend on what my mother says.

I no longer want to leave my dreams on the shelf.

"I see you've been working hard," said Claude. "Bravo. Before we go up in the sky, we're going to do some hands-on work. I'm going to show you how to make some nice paper airplanes . . ."

He really was crazy. And yet I was beginning to like him, and so, despite the oddness of the task, I set to and made them without a word.

"Well done!" Claude declared when I had finished. "We've got a real air force. Now we can get on board."

I followed him rather anxiously into the hot-air balloon's basket. When it began to rise, I clung to him.

"It's OK, Camille. Everything's going to be all right . . ."

Ashamed of myself, I stood up straight to control my fear and looked directly at the horizon. My stomach was still doing somersaults, but I kept my eyes wide open to make sure I missed nothing. I could feel my heart pounding and wondered if I would get vertigo.

"Be aware of everything you are feeling so that you can describe it in a while, OK?"

I kept hold of Claude's arm during the entire ascent, which was almost completely smooth. In the end, I was surprised to find I felt less vertigo than I had been expecting. I was still conscious of the pull of the void, my throat was dry, and my hands were shaking, but I was there and I was coping.

It was an incredible experience, and the view was to die for. It was so beautiful it brought tears to my eyes. Above all, I was becoming aware of what I was doing. I was capable of rising five hundred feet into the air and of overcoming my fears! I was filled with an elated sense of pride, which brought to my face a smile that I could not suppress.

"Anchor yourself, Camille, anchor yourself!" Claude whispered to me.

Seeing that I didn't understand, he explained the principle of "positive anchoring," a technique that allows you to recover at will the physical and emotional feelings you experienced at a particular happy moment.

First I had to anchor myself to a moment like that. Then to associate a word, image, or gesture to that sense of peace and happiness. Today in the balloon, I decided I would pinch the little finger on my left hand.

From then on, with training, I would be able to recover my anchor whenever I needed it by reproducing the gesture associated with this first moment, and at the same time recover the same positive emotional state.

I still felt I should ask Claude for a more specific explanation of how to do this, to make sure I had understood. So, in detail: in order to feel again this sense of peace and confidence, I needed to recover the memory of that moment of intense emotion. By placing myself alone in a calm and comfortable spot, focused but relaxed, and even with my eyes closed if that helped, I could conjure up a mental picture by revisiting that special memory, visualizing the scene once more and immersing myself in the physical and emotional sensations I had felt then. At that point, I could repeat the associated gesture (pinching my little finger, in this case) so as to intensify the wave of positive emotions.

"You should practice it often to make sure the anchoring is effective," Claude told me.

I was still slightly skeptical but promised I would try.

"The time has come to launch all your little airplanes overboard," he went on, "and to say farewell once and for all to all that weight. The symbolism of the gesture is very important..."

While he looked on encouragingly, I launched my paper planes into the air one by one. All of a sudden, I felt liberated. By throwing out these things I no longer wanted, I was reinforcing my determination to change. I had switched on the process of transformation, even if I didn't yet fully grasp all the consequences. One thing was for sure, though: it was too late now to go back. I would have to accept the challenge! For the moment, I watched joyfully as my little bits of paper glided through the air; I even waved them good-bye. *Take that, you useless burdens. Be very afraid: you're history.* I was really enjoying myself.

WHEN WE WERE BACK on terra firma, Claude suggested we go for a coffee.

"Well, Camille, are you proud of yourself?"

"Yes, I think so . . ."

"You can do better than that."

"YES! I'm proud of myself," I cried with more conviction.

"That's better," he said, adding some hot water to the coffee he'd been served. "The best way to bolster your self-esteem is to learn to be your own best friend. You have to value yourself, to have compassion for and to be kind to yourself, to show yourself gratitude as often as possible. Will you promise to do that for me?"

"I can try. But won't I have a swollen head afterward?" I joked.

"In your case, there's room for it," he immediately shot back. "And speaking of that, for the start of next week I want you to send me a list of all your best qualities, everything you're good at, all the successes you've had in your life. Can you do that?"

"Is that all? I'm warning you, it could be a very short list."

"Ah, Camille, Camille . . . If you start all that again, I'll make you start at square one. OK, OK, at first you might find it hard, but the more your brain is trained to look for the positive within you, the easier it will become. It really will, I promise. Oh, and I wanted to give you this."

He searched in his pocket and took out a small box. That made me laugh to myself—from a distance someone might think he was offering me a beautiful ring and asking me to marry him. Oddly, I found that thought exciting. But it wasn't a ring; it was a lovely yellow lotus. The second charm. So Claude thought I had reached the second level of change. I had difficulty hiding the flush of pride surging in me and bringing color to my cheeks. My eyes were shining as I thanked him and added the pendant to the first one on the necklace.

Claude received a call, which meant he had to leave quickly. Before going, he slipped a small piece of paper into my hand and then walked off without looking back. What a strange man.

"Everything is change, not to no longer be, but to become what is not yet." Epictetus. What if you drew me a portrait of the Camille you would like to be?

Until very soon,
Claude

... *nine* ...

The Camille-work-in-progress was hard at it.

Claude had asked me for a list of everything I was good at and the successes I felt I had known in my life, so over the following days I spent my free time in a kind of introspective exploration, probing the depths of my soul and my memories to unearth the raw materials he was looking for.

Positive experiences, personal qualities . . . At first, nothing more than a black hole. But then, little by little, they returned to the surface and took shape before my eyes.

To help guide me, I kept referring to the list of qualities that Claude had sent. I wondered which ones best described me:

Adventurous, agreeable, ambitious, astute, audacious, autonomous, calm, combative, conciliatory, confident, creative, dedicated, diplomatic, direct, disciplined, discreet, dynamic, efficient, empathetic, energetic,

extroverted, faithful, flexible, generous, gentle,
hardworking, honest, imaginative, independent,
innovative, intelligent, intuitive, jovial, just, leader,
methodical, motivated, multitasking, obliging,
observant, obstinate, open-minded, optimist,
organized, original, painstaking, patient, persevering,
polite, precise, prudent, pugnacious, punctual,
reserved, responsible, rigorous, self-controlled,
sensitive, serious, sociable, spontaneous, stable,
strategist, strong, stubborn, team player, tenacious,
tolerant, willful.

Agreeable, yes. Ambitious, not enough! Conciliatory, a little too much. Creative: I used to be. Sensitive, yes, no getting away from it. Serious and hardworking, out of necessity. Generous, empathetic . . . yes, to some extent.

As for the most successful events in my life—apart from the birth of my son, of course, there hadn't been that many. Maybe the occasion when I had gotten an A+ in art and my teacher had congratulated me so warmly and told me I ought to carry on, that I was talented. It still made me happy to remember that. Yes, then I had felt really appreciated. There was also the day when I had earned my business studies degree and told my mother the good news on the phone. But was that really my pleasure, or my mother's? I would have to talk about it with Claude.

As for the portrait of the Camille I would like to become, for the moment it was only a rough sketch. I wrote down all the ideas that occurred to me and sensed that even if it was all still unfocused, the process had begun and things were bound to become clearer.

As I continued with this excavation of my identity, nearly every day Claude sent me hints and tips to help me move toward the virtuous circle.

So it came as no surprise when, barely ten minutes after I had woken up, I heard my mobile buzz and found he had sent me another text message.

Good morning, Camille. Today you are to fill your day with humor and cheerfulness. That makes it easier to confront any little obstacles. Try pulling faces in front of the mirror: it's good for your morale and helps ward off wrinkles. Pull your tongue in all directions and shout, "Whaaa!" Mimic great sadness and great joy like Marcel Marceau, pronounce all your vowels in an exaggerated way, have fun! Spk soon, Claude.

I smiled. His exercise intrigued me, but it seemed a bit odd for me to be clowning about in the bathroom. At first I was very hesitant but gradually managed to relax, until finally I really let rip. My son was watching me from the doorway, unable to believe his eyes.

"What on earth are you doing, Mom?"

"Gymnastics for plastic surgery," I replied without missing a beat.

My reply astounded him, but children have an amazing ability to take on board the weirdest ideas.

"It looks like fun," he said seriously, like a judge on a talent show. "Can I try?"

I invited him to join me, and soon we were miming—with our faces—a high-wire double act. Adrien was incredibly good at it, and so I had no hesitation awarding him the clown first prize. He was so pleased at this that he was in a good mood all through breakfast, which for once we ate together, chatting the whole time. It had been ages since we'd done that.

Yes, Claude was right. It did you a lot of good to start your day with a bit of laughter and fun!

On another day, he suggested I try the game of the "imaginary camera," an exercise he had invented to help me change the way I looked at my reality by changing my "perception filter."

"When you go out, instead of focusing on sights that are unpleasant, ugly, or irritating, fix your attention on pleasant things. Take imaginary photos of happy coincidences in the street, on public transport, wherever you walk."

So now I had to train myself to be on the lookout for Beauty. It turned out to be quite a revelation. Rather than inevitably turning my gaze to beggars, grumpy passersby, or howling babies, I found myself staring at the sky, the pretty bird making its nest, a loving couple embracing, a mother caressing her child, a man helping an old lady carry her suitcase down the Métro steps, or listening to the soft rustle of foliage.

This new way of looking enchanted me. Each day I added to my collection of positive images, a photo album that was going to allow me to create a different view of the world.

... ten ...

As the weeks passed and I could sense that the symptoms of my acute routinitis were slowly but surely fading, I began to really believe in Claude's method. What convinced me above all was his two-pronged approach: the idea of working on the basic problem (Who am I? What do I really want?) at the same time as the symptoms (my self-image, my relation to the world and other people).

Have you noticed how the image you have of the world becomes more beautiful if you have a good self-image? Unfortunately, on this last point I still had a long way to go, because I could not get over my issues with self-esteem. Every day the sight of myself in the mirror cast a shadow over my mood. I was a stern judge of myself, examining my reflection from all angles, and was scornful of the extra weight I seemed doomed to carry around forever.

It wasn't too bad when I was standing. The buttons did up. It was sitting down when I felt guilty. Whenever the spare tire risked protruding over the size 8 I'd been too optimistic about ...

Sometimes I tried to kid myself that the trousers had shrunk or that the skirt was meant to be tight. But the evidence was plain for me to see: the vise was tightening around me. Besides, I had launched that little paper plane from a hot-air balloon. I had sworn in black and white that I didn't want to be carrying round those extra pounds with me anymore. It was a promise I had to keep.

So I made another appointment with Claude to discuss it.

I had been waiting for fifteen minutes when the door opened. For once, Claude looked in a hurry.

"Ah, Camille, come in. How are you? I'm sorry, I don't have much time for you today: I'm fitting you in between two meetings."

"It's very kind of you, Claude. I just need your advice about my goal to lose weight."

He listened to me absentmindedly, more concerned with tidying up the files strewn all over his desk. When he turned to put them in a cabinet, a sheet of paper fell from one of them. I got to my feet to pick it up. It was odd: a design for a building with lots of calculations and notes. I handed it to him. He took it from me, muttering his thanks. He seemed out of sorts.

"Are you all right, Claude? You seem preoccupied. I can come back another day, if you prefer."

"No, no, everything's fine, Camille. I've got a lot on my plate and I'm feeling a bit overwhelmed, that's all," he reassured me with a smile.

He put away the files as best he could—I was amazed how

many of them there were. Could he really have so many clients? Did routinology have so many followers?

He came and sat down again, automatically stroking his beard in the way a woman might run her hand through her hair: to regain his composure.

"Fine . . . well then, are you ready to go on a diet? Good. The key to achieving your objective is to frame it properly before you begin. Do you know the 'SMART method'?"

"No, I—"

"You need to make sure that your objective is S for Specific (you have to avoid it being vague) and M for Measurable—in this case, for example, success would be losing ten pounds. Then there's A for Attainable, defined as being achievable, thanks to a series of short steps; it mustn't be an 'unreachable star.' R for Realistic: to keep you motivated, your objective has to make sense in relation to your personality and your possibilities. And, finally, T for Timely: you need to set yourself a deadline."

As he described the method to me, I saw myself as a sculptor like Barbara Hepworth, imaginary chisel in hand, sculpting, shaping, creating my perfect objective. I drove the image from my mind to concentrate on reality.

"Does all that seem clear, Camille?"

"Yes, yes, completely."

"I'll give you a few minutes, then, to draw up your SMART objective. I'll be back."

He smiled and left the room. I got up and went to search for a piece of paper and a pencil in the same writing desk I had used at our first meeting. The sheet of paper was easy enough, but the pencils had been put away. Mechanically, I opened the drawer, and to my surprise found a framed photo. I recognized the background as Central Park in New York. Two men were posing for the photograph as if they were brothers. The contrast between them was striking: one exuded an air of self-assurance, strength, and success. The other, in spite of his height, seemed almost fragile. A giant with feet of clay. His eyes seemed clouded by a raft of shadows. He had a family likeness to Claude but must have weighed forty-five pounds more! Perhaps he was his brother?

Hearing steps in the corridor, I quickly shut the drawer.

"How's it going, Camille?"

"Oh, fine, I just need a pencil."

"You should have taken one. Here, use this."

"Thanks," I stammered, embarrassed at my tactless curiosity.

The entire time I was considering my SMART objective, I was wondering who the man in the photo could have been. I resolved to ask Claude at some point.

Half an hour later, I left with my objective under my arm and with ten pounds to lose under my belt. By this stage I was as motivated as Mother Teresa. I thought it was going to be— pardon the expression—a piece of cake. However, I was not taking into account the cold war that kitchens can declare.

... eleven ...

Over the next few days, I summoned up the strength to put my good resolutions into practice.

"Just saying the word 'diet' makes one put on weight," Claude had warned me. "You need to learn to find pleasure elsewhere."

That was a good one. As if anyone had ever found pleasure in steamed broccoli or broiled fish!

"Think about spices, Camille."

Why not, after all? What had I got to lose? (Apart from a few pounds . . .) So I raided the local supermarket and came back with an armful of spices that would add flavor and, I hoped, raise the troops' morale. Garlic, coriander, turmeric, paprika, curry powder, garam masala. And gray, black, and white pepper: I didn't care what color it was, provided the taste was intoxicating. The enemy was tastelessness.

In the cold war of hot food, I learned how to use the secret weapons of healthy eating. The trick of using fat-free yogurt; the heroic part white meats could play in my special dishes.

Low fat, that was the challenge, because there were enemies lurking in every dark corner of the cupboard: cans of Pringles and shortbread cookies lying in ambush, waiting slyly for their moment of glory.

Their greatest ally? My own son! There was no way I could sacrifice his appetite on the altar of my good intentions. So I had to suffer and carry on buying all those forbidden fruits that he wolfed down so innocently in front of me, while I stoically ate an apple.

But the worst hour of the day was not his snack time. No, that came at nightfall, when the call of the wine rack became pressing, even irresistible. The danger of a calorie bomb attack was at its height. Temptations rained down on me, threatening to destroy all my best intentions. And what about the Macaroni Syndrome? It was as perverse as its cousin from Stockholm, leading me to sympathize with the enemy, to do a deal with my conscience: just a tiny spoonful to finish up my boy's plate . . .

Even so, my bravery paid off. In a few days I could already see some real improvements. Encouraged by these early victories, I held fast, silently muttering to myself the hymn of the slimming experts to the glory of lower fat, less sugar, reduced salt . . .

Alas, hardly had the trumpets of victory begun to sound than an enemy I had underestimated mounted a counterattack: boredom.

In the office, we were going through a lean patch, and my boss preferred to give what work there was to my full-time colleagues. Each hour seemed like 360 minutes, maybe even 500. Sometimes 1,000. I could hardly wait for the four o'clock break. In other words, I was stagnating.

It was then of course that the idea of surrendering raised its pointy little head. What if I forgot my diet just this once? Just for today? Who would ever know?

I went down to the vending machine, that little shop of calorific horrors. Just a tiny bar of something . . . After all, where was the harm? I was just about to slip a coin into the slot when my mobile began to vibrate. It was a text message from Claude. How was it possible? Did he have a sixth sense or something? I cursed him under my breath.

How are things? Are you bearing up?

I replied with a casual lie:

Of course. Fab. Have a good afternoon. Cam.

He'll never know, he'll never know, I kept telling myself as I turned back to the machine, money in hand. But it was too late. I could feel Claude's presence all around me, as if his eyes were prying into everything. *Big Brother is watching you!* I was living the diet version of *1984*.

Thwarted, with one last sad glance at the machine, I dragged my feet back to my desk. I opened my drawer, where a packet of almonds awaited me. I allowed myself five, plus an apple. Binge-ing like an ant.

Then suddenly a sense of revolt surged within me. His advice about "health and well-being" was starting to get on my nerves. Nothing but the worst hypocrisy.

> Take the stairs instead of the elevator, go out for a walk at lunchtime, *blah.* You can also firm your buttocks sitting down: you simply have to clench and then relax them discreetly, *blah blah.* Bored waiting for the Métro? Stand on tiptoe, then lower your heels down again! As for your abs, why not pull your stomach in whenever you pass a door, *blah blah blah*? Easy-peasy. *Yada yada yada . . .*

Yes, I know. Doubtless I'd reached the resistance stage. But who wouldn't feel rebellious at the idea of giving up all those sweet temptations paraded in front of us all the time? Nonetheless, I needed to take care if I didn't want to feel like a hopeless failure when it came to filling in my "Promises Notebook": another of Claude's ideas to make me more committed to my resolutions and avoid any backsliding. For every promise I made myself, he told me I had to tick the box "kept" or "not kept." And there was no way I was going to see him in a few days' time with a long list of "not kept"s in the book.

I was thinking about all this when my dear colleague Franck (in reality, my office enemy number one) called out, "Are you OK, Camille? You've got a very strange look on your face."

"Oh, yes, everything's fine . . . I'm trying to concentrate, that's all."

"Ah, it's just that you look as if you're about to lay an egg."

Ha-ha. Very funny.

There was no way I was going to tell him I was clenching my buttocks. He never missed an opportunity to bait me anyway.

"Talking of eggs, take a look at the top of your head."

Take that! One all, Baldy. From the way his cheeks flushed, I could tell I'd hit home. I wasn't very proud of myself, but he shouldn't have started it. He was forever going at me, and I always dreaded his jibes. I would have to talk to Claude about it.

As if there were some telepathic link between us, at that very moment I got a chat request on my computer.

—Well, Camille, how's your "mind over body" exercise going?

—Not bad . . . Sometimes it's hard to resist temptation though.

—But you have?

—Yes.

—Good! Don't forget to write that down in your Positive Notebook. Have I mentioned that to you already?

—No, not yet . . .

—Ah, it's very important. Buy a small address book and jot down in alphabetical order all your triumphs, big and small, and all the things that make you happy, big and small. Soon you'll have a whole collection of positive anchoring. You'll see; it's excellent for your self-esteem and personal satisfaction.

—Interesting! OK, Claude, I'll think about it.

I saw the little pencil icon wobbling, showing he was busy writing me a long reply. A ping told me he had finished:

—I'm counting on you to not simply pay lip service to this. Each resolution has to count. Many people know what they're supposed to do to lead a happy life but never really put it into practice. It's not always easy to keep one's promises. Laziness, tiredness, discouragement are all enemies lying in wait. But keep going: it will be worth it!

I took his word for it.

... twelve ...

When I left work that day I passed by a bookshop and remembered Claude's advice. I thought the idea of a Positive Notebook was great. Why not give it a try? At the very least it would give me something to do in front of the TV. I went in and chose a pocket-sized one that would be easy to slip into my coat or purse, so that it would always be handy. My day had been so empty, it was exhausting. I couldn't wait to get home and relax.

But I'd forgotten what the atmosphere there was really like.

No sooner had I crossed the threshold then icy tension hit me. Adrien was having one of his off days and barely said hello. The girl I employed to look after him and help with his homework didn't seem to be in a much better mood. Glancing at the schoolbooks lined up in ranks on the living-room table, I guessed the reason for the chill. Charlotte never needed any encouragement to complain about my son's lack of attention and motivation. He fidgeted the whole time, got up on any pretext—he wanted something to eat, to drink, or to blow his nose or go to the bathroom; he invented a stream of excuses to put off the moment when he really got down to work. She accompanied her diatribe with irritated blinking and a disapproving pursing of the lips. I thanked her for her lucid debriefing while at the same time sighing wearily at the prospect of taking over from her.

A quarter of an hour later, I had already reached the end of my patience. Entrenched in his preteen logic, Adrien blamed Charlotte: she was useless at explaining things, and besides, he didn't like her. Seeing that his arguments weren't having any great effect, he changed tack and said that he just couldn't manage it all—his teacher gave them far too much homework.

I should have seen that the poor kid had had more than he could take, but I was feeling the same way, and so all I could think of was to punish him by not allowing him any time on his tablet. He ran off into his bedroom, slamming the door behind him. I had to use all my diplomatic skills to calm things down and get him to come back to his homework.

When Sebastien arrived, I was trying to make dinner with one hand, holding a workbook open in the other, while getting Adrien to recite the wretched lesson. Sebastien gave me a peck on the cheek and asked if I'd had a good day without so much as looking at me. I think that if I'd replied, "No, it was dreadful actually, thanks for asking," he wouldn't have noticed.

I could sense the pressure building but tried my best to ignore it. Adrien found it hard to learn things by heart—he picked things up quickly but was intuitive rather than methodical—and with every line he stumbled over, I could feel my calm evaporating. I was a perfectionist, and I found his sloppiness intolerable.

Sebastien reappeared from the bedroom, his shirt open and half outside his trousers. He headed straight for the bathroom.

"I don't believe it! What on earth is this mess?" he shouted as soon as he went in. "Who did this?"

"Not me!" retorted Adrien.

A typical knee-jerk preteen response. I felt obliged to intervene.

"Sorry, it must have been me, Seb. I was really running late this morning."

The growl of a bear in the depths of the apartment.

Charming!

He came back into the living room carrying his laptop and immediately flew off the handle again.

"Why are there crumbs all over the sofa? Adrien! How many times have I told you not to have your snack there!"

I abandoned my cooking pot and workbook and went to join Sebastien. I was fed up with him arriving stressed out and cross like this; it was becoming a habit. Nonetheless, I tried to calm things down.

"Don't worry, I'll see to it," I said.

"No, I'LL do it," he replied curtly.

Here we go again . . .

Sighing deeply, he brushed off the crumbs, then stretched out on the sofa with his computer.

He had taken off his socks, and for some reason the sight of his toenails wiggling about on the coffee table under my nose irritated me still further. Or maybe it was his complete indifference to the domestic battle I was going to have to deal with before I had the chance to sit down. I usually let things go, but that evening it was all too much for me. I had to say something.

"Are you OK? I'm not disturbing you, am I?"

"What's the matter now?" he snapped.

"I can't imagine . . . except that perhaps I might need a bit of help?"

"What are you going at me for?"

"Oh, for God's sake, I'm not going at you, I was simply asking you to pay me some attention!"

"And now you're shouting at me? Thanks, that's really great at the end of a hard day's work! Have you paid *me* any attention since I got here?"

"Well, that's just the goddamn limit! You're going at me for looking after your son?"

"There you go again, shouting at me!"

Seeing a storm brewing, Adrien slipped away into his room, delighted at avoiding his homework.

"Right, that's it. I've had enough of doing everything myself!"

"Oh, I see. You're having one of your usual little hissy fits."

"What? You swan in here, ignore me and Adrien, start pissing around on the computer with your little virtual friends . . ."

"Do you really think I had such a great time today? I've been working like a dog, I had three meetings back-to-back, I—"

"You mean I haven't been working?"

"OK, yes, you do work," he said condescendingly.

"What are you implying? That working four days a week isn't the same, or what?"

"I never said that!"

"You might as well have!" I cried. I was at the end of my tether. "I've had it. Let's see how you get on without me. I'm taking off my apron. Handing in my notice."

"That's it, quit, why don't you? Why don't we get divorced while we're at it? It seems as though that's what you want!"

His words struck me like a boomerang in midflight. Sobbing, I picked up my coat and left the apartment, slamming the door behind me.

... *thirteen* ...

Out in the street, I looked up at our windows and saw my son's sad face. He drew a heart in the air aimed at me, as if he thought it was his fault Sebastien and I had quarreled. His gesture almost made me cry. I smiled back up at him, and then I set off for a walk: I needed to calm down.

I was hoping I wouldn't bump into any neighbors. I didn't want anyone to see me like this. *But that's ridiculous, worrying about what other people think at a time like this.* Still, I avoided looking any passersby in the eye; I was sure my distress was obvious in my face, and I didn't want them to see. No witnesses to my depression, please.

I walked to a small square and called Claude.

"Claude? Camille here . . . Am I disturbing you?" I asked through my sniffles.

I didn't have to tell him I was in trouble: he guessed that straightaway.

"It's Sebastien; we've had a fight. I couldn't take it anymore. It's as if there's a . . . a gulf between us."

I told him everything, and it did me good to sense that he was listening so closely to my woes. What luxury to have such a receptive ear.

"He seems completely incapable of offering me anything I need."

"And what *do* you need?" Claude shot back.

"I don't know . . . I need him to pay attention to me, to be kind and thoughtful. But instead of that, it's like having a robot in the apartment. He does nothing but moan and then hide behind his computer, in his own little world. I even get jealous of his virtual friends! While he's online, everything around him could collapse and he wouldn't notice! And in the meantime I have to be everywhere, looking after Adrien, his homework, cooking dinner. It's not fair!"

"I understand, Camille . . ."

"On top of that, he's forever telling me I don't listen to him. But that's not true. He's the one who won't listen! I can't get a word in; he brings everything back to himself."

I was pacing up and down the deserted square, my nerves still jangling.

"Ah yes, the 'he's-the-one-who' game. That's not good! In fact, that's why you can't hear each other: it's like two deaf people talking. If you're listening unwillingly it means you're not listening at all. To really listen, you have to be able to identify with what the other person is experiencing, to have empathy. You can't imagine how rare it is to find someone who truly knows how to listen. I often tell myself that whoever knows that will be the king of this world. Camille, remember that in an argument not everything is as it seems: you have to learn to read between the lines to uncover the real emotions. Behind a criticism there may be fear; behind aggression there could be sadness or an unhealed wound."

As I listened to him, I drew my coat closer around me. I suddenly felt cold—all these swirling emotions . . .

"But it's so *hard* to listen sympathetically. You should see how he looks at me when we're arguing. I get the dreadful feeling that . . . that he doesn't love me!"

"Mmm . . . That's interesting. How about replacing that 'he' with 'I'?"

I was too taken aback to say a word.

"Yes, you heard me correctly."

"I . . . You mean *I* don't love myself?"

"Yes, that's it, Camille. You tend to interpret your partner's behavior through the lens of your own negative thoughts. And that distorts everything. Right now you don't love yourself very much, because you've got it into your head that you are less pretty with those few extra pounds and your first little wrinkles. You unconsciously project onto your husband your fear that you are no longer someone to be loved. And if you carry on like that, it'll become a self-fulfilling prophecy! You'll have confirmed your worst-case scenario: you're no longer desirable, and so he doesn't love you anymore."

His words slowly seeped into my mind, but the soothing effect they had was cut short by the arrival of two men in the park. They had hoods pulled up over their heads, and warily, I watched them approach. I had been so desperate to hear what Claude had to say that it had not occurred to me it might be unwise to hang around at night in this deserted square. I quickly made my way toward the exit, trying not to give the impression I was running away. All of a sudden I felt a hand on my shoulder. I cried out and swiveled to break free of his grasp. One of the two men leaned toward me. He was young and reeked of weed.

"You've dropped something," he said, holding out the scarf I usually tie round the strap of my bag.

"Ah . . . thanks so much," I stammered, almost snatching it from him. Then I rushed away.

At the other end of the line, Claude was getting worried.

"Hello, Camille? Hello, are you still there?"

Swiftly back on the well-lit streets of my own neighborhood, I waited for my heart rate to subside before I answered him.

"I'm sorry, Claude, just a little . . . incident. What were you saying?"

In order to illustrate what was going on when we argued, he outlined the principle of the "dramatic triangle." He explained how, in this negative scenario, each person in a relationship could successively play the role of victim, persecutor, and savior.

"And the problem is that there can never be any positive resolution, unless you quit the game altogether. In your case, here's what happens: he is the persecutor, because he moans the whole time; you're the savior when you offer to sweep up the crumbs, but then the victim when you complain he doesn't help you. Next, you become the persecutor by criticizing him for his behavior, and it's his turn to be the victim when he complains what a frightful day he's had, and so on. Each of you swaps roles, unable to find any other way out than the inevitable full-blown argument! But there *are* ways of getting out of the triangle . . ."

"What are they? Quick, tell me!"

"First of all, you need to recognize what's going on in order to put a stop to the game and wait for a calmer moment when you can renew the dialogue. Second, clearly identify your needs so that you can ask your partner directly and he can see without a decoder what it is you want. If it's legitimate and reasonable, there's no reason he shouldn't agree."

"That's interesting . . ."

I pressed the mobile to my ear, trying to ignore the fact that my fingertips were freezing. I changed hands and thrust the free one as deep as I could into my coat pocket.

"You'll also have to set your limits and tell everyone around you what they are," Claude went on. "You're a people pleaser: that means you're always trying to satisfy the other person's wishes and you end up sacrificing your own. You're full of empathy—and of course it's a good thing to be concerned about someone else's well-being. But don't confuse 'dry empathy' with 'wet empathy.' In the latter, you take on board the other person's drama; you absorb their negative emotions and end up in a bad way yourself. Dry empathy, on the other hand, means you manage to hear and share the problems of those around you but you don't let yourself get contaminated by their dark thoughts. You put up a protective shield that stops you getting dragged down—which is very useful! Not to mention the fact that eventually, thanks to feeling that you have to be a 'good egg' all the time, you end up blowing a fuse. That's what happened tonight, wasn't it?"

I agreed.

"Don't worry. You simply have to make adjustments. Stop being too nice; simply be true to your emotions. And another important thing: learn to 'steam off stamps' as you go along, rather than exploding like a pressure cooker, the way you did just now."

"Steam off stamps? What does that mean? You want me to write to him?"

"No, not at all! Steaming off stamps is an expression that means you should show what you're feeling as you go along. You need to tell your husband what's upsetting you when it happens."

"OK . . ."

"If you tell him *nicely,* there's no reason for him not to

listen. Then in the future, when you sense that things are coming to a boil, you can agree with him on a 'red card.'"

"A red card?"

"Yes. You two need to find a signal to warn the other there's a danger of things turning into an argument. My wife and I do that, and it works wonderfully. It's like in a car when a red light comes on: you know there's danger ahead. And if you're both aware of it, then you can avoid an escalation into aggression."

A ping. Another call on my mobile. It must be Sebastien. Should I pick up or not? Not immediately. I sent a text:

I'm on a call.

"Camille, are you still there? I heard a ping."

"Yes, yes, it was another call. It's not urgent. I'll ring back."

"Was it your husband?"

"Yes, but please, go on. This is such good stuff."

"OK, Camille. But I'll be quick: you need to get home, and I have a good book waiting for me by my fire."

I hadn't realized I had kept him on the phone for so long. I felt embarrassed.

"One last thing that's important, Camille: you have to learn to criticize without being aggressive. That means you shouldn't start your sentences with those 'you' accusations. They're fatal. I call them 'reproach machine guns': they're bound to make the other person blow a fuse. What you need to do is move your FEET."

"What's this got to do with footwork?"

"They're initials: F, you remind him of the Facts that have upset you. E, you express your Emotions, what you felt at the time. E, you Encourage him, and T, you call a Truce. That way, it's a win-win situation for both of you. If we take your argument tonight, it would mean something like: 'When you hinted that I worked less than you (the *Fact*), I was upset because I felt you didn't value me (the *Emotion*), when I really need you to support and feel proud of me, just as no doubt you do. I think we should give each other tokens of our appreciation more often so that we both feel valued for the contribution we make to the family (the *Encouragement* that's constructive for both sides). That should help put a stop to difficulties and misunderstandings (the *Truce*). What do you think?"

"Not bad. But people don't really behave like that."

"What's more important? Behaving naturally or avoiding a hideous fight?"

I smiled to myself.

"OK, Claude, I get the idea. But how am I going to sort things out right now? When I left him, he was in a rage. He even mentioned divorce!"

"Bah, that was just his anger talking . . . I'm sure that if you offer him the hand of reconciliation he won't refuse it. To take a step toward the other person seems so simple, and yet so few people do it. That's why there are so many divorces. It's such a shame! All that wasted love when with a little effort those relationships could be so successful. Although of course, in our hyperconsumerist society, we find it easier to throw things away than to repair them. 'Great joys come from heaven, little joys from effort,' as that Chinese proverb says."

"Oh, Claude, sometimes I get so sad. I feel as though the glass is always half empty."

"There you go again. Your mind keeps sending you negative images. But remember, you can decide it's got to change!"

"How do I do that?"

"For a start, continue to do what we've been doing up to now: feeling good about yourself, taking care of yourself, recentering yourself on your good qualities and attributes, rediscovering your needs and core values. In other words, flourishing from within. You shouldn't make your husband feel he is the only one responsible for your happiness. He should be more like the cherry on the cake in your life."

I got a weird mental image of Sebastien's head stuck on top of a huge cake oozing cream. Scary.

"You think I expect too much of him?"

"It's not for me to answer that question. I'm simply saying that you need to know how to live at a proper distance. It's like an elastic band: if it's too tight, it's restrictive; if it's too loose, everything falls apart. You need it to have the right tension. But we also need to untangle all the knots tying us to the past."

"Meaning?"

"Meaning in your case that you need to understand how the relationships you had as a child continue to influence your life today."

"I don't see how something that happened in the past can influence my life now."

"Oh, but you can't imagine how much it does! Didn't you tell me that your father left your mother before you were two?"

"Yes, that's right."

"It's possible that certain situations in your present life re-awaken those wounds and—despite yourself—unleash an emotional reaction out of all proportion to what's caused it. That's what I mean by 'elastic bands.' Tonight, unconsciously, you stretched things so far that your partner was driven to say that you would end up divorcing. Without being aware of it, you have reinforced an old negative pattern, one that terrified you as a child: being abandoned by the man you love."

"But that's terrible! I honestly didn't realize . . ."

By now I was completely frozen, and so I went into a bar that was still open and ordered a hot chocolate. My mobile was warm in my hands: I had been talking to Claude for a good half hour, and he was still coaching with the same enthusiasm as always. He must have lived through all this himself at some point, surely: it came out so naturally. And I didn't want to miss a word of it.

"Becoming aware is an excellent first step to cutting those ties to the past. After that, by continuing to work on yourself and by embracing positive change you'll be able to banish those old demons once and for all. You're no longer the helpless little girl you were when your father walked out. You're a responsible, autonomous adult, able to face up to whatever life throws at you.

Even so, it's important to reassure that part of you that is frightened and that suffered in the past. If you do, you'll become reconciled to that important piece of yourself."

"So how do you reassure the little girl inside you?" I asked, blowing on my steaming hot chocolate.

"You sit down quietly in a corner and talk to her gently, the way you do with your own child. You can tell her you love her, that you'll always be there, that she can rely on you . . . But to get over that childhood wound completely, you'll have to go through the forgiveness stage."

"Which is?"

"You'll have to forgive your father."

I was so stunned I didn't know what to say.

Claude must have sensed my difficulty, because he went on, trying to soften the blow. "You can do that when the moment comes, when you're ready for it. For now, concentrate on your relationship with your husband: make it work, give more!"

"Doesn't that take us back to square one? Why do I always have to be the one to make an effort? Why not him?"

"Because your positive input into the relationship will reap rich rewards. Doing good to others is enlightened self-interest, according to Aristotle. Besides, don't forget that, for now, you are ahead of him in terms of personal development. So you have to show him the way. Maybe it's a fact, also, that it comes more naturally to you to take the initiative? You'll know instinctively how to strike the spark to rekindle the fire . . . Don't you agree it's better to stop fighting over 'who did what'? To stop trying to make out which one of the two of you is more deserving?"

Yes, of course. He was right. A hundred times over.

"Start from the principle that the other person is trying to give as much as he can at any given moment in a relationship. Then concentrate on what he is bringing that is positive, rather than focusing on what disappoints you because it doesn't completely live up to your expectations. You reap what you sow: that old adage makes sense. If you sow criticism, you reap resentment and disillusionment. Sow love and appreciation, and you'll reap tenderness and gratitude."

"Mmm . . . I can see that, but what drives me mad is how *lukewarm* he is. Our love life is so . . . so *uninspiring* now! No passion or . . . or romantic gestures. I miss those . . ."

"Well, you have to find a middle way there too: no unattainable fantasies, but no lowering of your sights either. You're right to want to improve your love life—so long as you don't have unrealistic expectations. You have to respect and accept your partner's basic character and not expect from him things he can't give you. Love is like a plant that demands lots of care and grows best when it's watered. Appreciate your husband for everything he does well, show him how grateful you are, demonstrate your admiration. He'll flourish and will probably be much more receptive to your advances. So, smiles, support, tenderness: those are your three watchwords."

Another ping.

"That's Sebastien again."

"All right, answer him, Camille—what are you waiting for?"

"Claude?"

"Yes?"

"Thank you."

SEBASTIEN AND I EXCHANGED a few words, enough to relieve the tension. And to add a touch of humor to our reconciliation, when I got home I waved a white handkerchief in the doorway. Peace was sealed with a kiss.

Adrien took advantage to rush out of his hiding place and hug us.

"So you're not going to get a divorce?" he asked anxiously.

Sebastien and I searched each other's faces, looking for reassurance. And in his eyes I saw . . . yes . . . a glimmer of affection that comforted me.

"Of course not," I told Adrien, ruffling his mop of hair.

"Hey, Mom!" he protested, quickly smoothing his locks.

For some months now, he had been very concerned about his "look." Woe betide anyone touching his carefully gelled hairstyle! Then, quick to take advantage of the general air of reconciliation, the cunning little guy returned to the attack: "Now that I've finished all my homework, could I have some time on my tablet, Mommy?" looking up at me with his huge doe eyes.

I had no idea what profession he would end up in, but I

wasn't too worried about him. He had a real talent for making people do what he wanted them to. It was impossible to be cross with him for long, or to resist his charm offensive . . .

As soon as Adrien was busy with his tablet like a veteran gamer, I turned my attention to Sebastien. I was still upset about the argument, so I was struggling to be affectionate. And while he poured us the remains of a bottle of white, I realized how much work we were going to have to do to restore our love life to its former glory. Rebuilding Shangri-La was a long way off!

Fortunately, when it came to ways and means, it seemed Claude was aware of quite a few.

... fourteen ...

For my next well-being lesson, Claude had asked me to meet him in the children's amusement park at the Jardin d'Acclimatation. It was ages since I'd been there. I was like an overexcited child myself when I saw the carousel spinning round and the toffee apples being crunched. I would gladly have sinned with some chocolate doughnuts but, thank god, Claude arrived in the nick of time to save me from temptation. First of all he took me for tea at Angelina's, where I allowed myself a single treat: a slice of lemon tart—and given how stoic I was in resisting the displays of delicious cakes, that's worth pointing out. After that, Claude led me to the Hall of Mirrors.

"What do you see, Camille?"

"Oh my god! Myself even fatter and more grotesque," I said with a laugh.

"And is that a true image of you?"

"No, thank goodness! I'm not *that* fat."

"And you're not fat in real life either, Camille. Most of the time you see yourself in a funhouse mirror because all your negative thoughts distort reality. Your mind plays tricks on you. It tells you lies, and you end up believing them! Remember, though: you have the power to halt those thoughts, even to change them. Look at me, Camille: Who tells you what to think?"

"I don't know."

"Yes, you do."

"Me?"

"Of course. Nobody but you! Most of the time we're very poor judges of ourselves. You're convinced you are too fat because of those extra ten pounds, but it's only inside your head that this is such a huge problem. Ten pounds is no big deal, I can assure you!"

I glanced at him, recalling the man in the photo he kept in his desk. Was that someone close to him? Or perhaps it was *him*? I didn't dare ask him directly, so I tried a roundabout approach.

"I get the impression you know a lot about the subject . . ."

I saw his brow crease and a look of surprise flit across his face. He cleared his throat as if trying to gain time because my question embarrassed him. He looked away, and his reply was evasive: "Yes, I do know a lot about it."

"Because you've experienced it yourself?"

I could tell from his expression that my questions were bothering him.

"Possibly. But we're not here to talk about me."

That's a shame, I thought. I would really have liked to know more about his life but sensed that this was not the moment.

He led me back to the first mirror in the building: a normal one.

"So now, Camille, take a good look at yourself and tell me what you most like about your appearance."

I studied my reflection.

"Well, I quite like my eyes; they are lively and a nice color . . ."

"Great! Carry on."

I looked a bit lower to see what I thought of my body.

"My chest isn't bad either—I've got a decent cleavage. I like my ankles as well. My legs are slim below the knee!"

"That's perfect, Camille. Now you need to do all you can to focus your attention on your good points rather than on your tiny flaws, which no one really notices anyway. Never forget those women who weren't particularly pretty and yet were hugely sought after. Like Édith Piaf, for example; she had loads of lovers, and they were all really handsome. Or even Marilyn Monroe, who wasn't exactly skinny! What's most important—and I know you know this—is what comes from within. Self-confidence is your greatest asset. Shine and you'll be irresistible. If you're filled with beauty, you will be attractive—goodness and kindness sparkle far more than jewels. What's inside you is immediately obvious from the outside."

I felt like asking if this was what had happened in his case, but there was a veil of mystery hanging over his life that I didn't yet dare raise. I made do with a joke: "That sounds a bit like a yogurt ad, but I get the general idea."

"You need to work hard every day to become a better person. If you give off positive vibes, you'll soon see how successful you can be."

"What if I *can't* do it, Claude? What if despite everything I still think I'm fat and ugly?"

"Shhh! Stop 'feeding your rats,' Camille. By your rats I mean your fears, complexes, misconceptions, all that side of you that likes to complain and play the victim. Do you understand what's going on in your head when you do that?"

"Mmm . . . Maybe if I'm ugly I won't attract much attention, and so I won't run the risk of disappointing anyone. Or of being disappointed. That way at least people won't expect too much of me and leave me in peace."

"And what would be the risk in attracting attention?"

"If you attract more attention, you get commented on more, you're judged, and so you're more likely to get hurt."

"That's right, except that you can only be hurt if you're vulnerable. The more confidence you have in who you are, the less other people can hurt you. Once you have rebuilt your self-esteem, when you have a life project that properly suits your personality and beliefs, you'll no longer be afraid. Your positive attitude will buoy you; you'll be aligned, in harmony with yourself and the world."

"When you put it like that, it makes me want to try. I hope I can sort myself out soon."

"That depends entirely on you, Camille."

"So how do I improve my own self-image?"

Claude led me to a slimming mirror.

"For a start, every morning in front of your mirror you are going to change your 'inner dialogue.' You are to repeat words of encouragement. You are beautiful, attractive; you like your body; you have lovely eyes; you are a remarkable woman who achieves whatever she sets out to do, et cetera."

"Isn't that going a bit far?"

"No, it's barely the start!" Claude teased me. "After that, you need to learn the 'art of modeling yourself.'"

"What's that?"

"Which woman do you most admire, and why?"

"I don't know . . . Oh yes, I adore Audrey Hepburn. I think she had such charm and poise."

"Good. So you should study Audrey Hepburn, her demeanor, the way she walked, smiled . . . Learn to reproduce her gestures. Close your eyes. Visualize yourself walking down the street as if you were Audrey Hepburn. How do you feel?"

"Beautiful, sure of myself, grounded . . ."

"And how do the people around you react?"

"They look at me, admire me . . ."

"Does that feel good?"

"Very good!"

"Fantastic! Keep those feelings in your mind, and don't hesitate to do it for real. Get into the skin of one of your role models!"

"OK, I'll try. It could be fun."

"While we're talking of role models . . . whom do you most admire? What are their good qualities? What's their recipe for success? Study their lives, read their biographies. Make a collage of images using photos of them. Can you do that in the next two weeks?"

"Mmm . . . I'll give it a try."

In fact, I felt a bit like Adrien given too much homework by his teacher, but Claude had warned me those little inner monsters are always lying in wait: laziness, tiredness, discouragement . . . I had to apply myself, even if I thought that everything was moving too fast and I wasn't yet comfortable as the "new me."

... *fifteen* ...

I arrived home exhausted. All this new information was whirling around in my head. So many changes to make in such a short time! I needed a good bath to relax. I put in a ton of bubbles and slipped into the scalding water to play with the foam like I used to when I was a child: wonderful!

For once I had the time: the previous evening, rather than watch TV, I had gotten supper ready for tonight. All we had to do was sit down and eat.

The meal was a real treat and earned me a chorus of oohs and aahs of delight from my men's satisfied taste buds.

"It's wicked, Mom! You should go on *MasterChef*!"

I laughed to myself when I saw my son serving himself a third helping of the tart, in which I had slipped some silky tofu and zucchini with olives and slices of goat's cheese.

He's eating zucchini . . . He's eating zucchini . . .

It's true that it made a change from frozen food.

After supper Adrien often asked me to play a board game

with him, but I never felt up to it. Besides, wasn't I a bit old? When this time I said yes, his jaw dropped. The gleam of joy in his eyes, that unadulterated joy only children feel, swept away any remaining doubts.

Again, this was something Claude had suggested. To stop being too adult. To let myself go more in sharing moments with my son. "The secret is to join in," he had said, winking in complicity. So there I was trying to reconnect with my inner child, that playful, creative side of myself too often held in check by the adult, party-pooper side of my character. Against all expectations, I enjoyed myself. And my son's radiant face made it all worthwhile. With his need for play and for company fully satisfied, he went to bed without any fuss. Bingo!

"Come and have a cuddle," said Sebastien from the sofa when I rejoined him in the living room.

"A bit later," I replied gently. "I've got work to do."

He seemed surprised, even slightly taken aback. Maybe because it was usually me wanting physical contact. For once, the roles were reversed. Could it be I had found the right tension on our elastic band?

I sat at the table in the dining room with my laptop and some paper and pencils. I began with the simplest task: to make a list of the famous people I wanted to be like.

I wrote in a rush:

I'd like to have the wisdom of a Gandhi, the calm of a Buddha, the grace of an Audrey Hepburn, the business

acumen of a Rockefeller, the willpower and self-denial
of a Mother Teresa, the courage of a Martin Luther
King Jr., the deductive skill of a Sherlock Holmes,
the creative genius of a Picasso, the inventiveness
of a Steve Jobs, the visionary imagination of a
Leonardo da Vinci, the emotive power of a Chaplin,
and finally the composure and good nature of my
grandfather!

Pleased with my brainstorming, I searched for and then
printed photos of all these people to create the collage of my role
models. I had not been expecting to feel so good doing this exercise: all those faces inspired and revitalized me. Looking at
them, I tried to understand—as far as I could—the secret of
their talent, to learn just a little of the lesson of their success. I
found that this small exercise allowed me to highlight some of
my own good qualities and to focus more keenly on what kind
of person I wished to become.

The collage of my role models looked fantastic. I decided to
give it pride of place next to my desk. Then I continued to re-
search my favorite subject: the fashion world. I read biographies
of the great designers, including my all-time favorite: Jean Paul
Gaultier.

I avidly read his Wikipedia entry:

At the age of fifteen, he designed sketches of a
children's clothes collection. It was after seeing the

movie *Paris Frills* by Jacques Becker, for which Marcel
Rochas designed all the costumes, that he decided to
make fashion his profession. He sent a portfolio to Yves
Saint Laurent but was rejected. Next his sketches went
to Pierre Cardin. On the day of his eighteenth
birthday, he joined that fashion house, where he spent
a little under a year before moving on to the "madcap"
Jacques Esterel. In 1971, he joined Jean Patou.

How could such a talented man be rejected at the start of his
career by Yves Saint Laurent? Unbelievable. It reminded me of
the story about perseverance that my grandfather often used to
tell me:

"Do you know who this man is? He was born in poverty and
had to face defeat throughout his life. He could have given up
many times and found a thousand reasons for doing so, and yet
he didn't. He had the mind-set of a champion and in the end
became one. And a champion never gives up. As a child, he was
driven from his house. He lost his mother. Went bust for the first
time. Was defeated in the state legislative elections. Lost his job.
Went bust again and took seventeen years to pay off his debts.
His fiancée died. He suffered a serious nervous breakdown. Was
defeated as chairman of the House of Representatives in Illinois,
then elected to Congress, but not reelected. He was never ap-
pointed to the post of county surveyor in his native state, although he applied for it many times. He ran for the United States
Senate but lost. Was a candidate for the vice presidency at his

party's national convention and won fewer than a hundred votes. He ran for the Senate again and was beaten again . . . That man, Camille, was President Abraham Lincoln!"

He always smiled as he came to his punch line.

What about me? Had I persevered throughout my life or had I given up too quickly on my dreams? That thought soured my mood. Disgruntled, I went to the closet at the end of the hallway and took out my portfolio. I silently flicked through the designs I had drawn years earlier as a student. I was astonished to see how freely I drew: I had a real talent back then. Maybe I could have done something with it, if I'd gone to art school rather than taken up business studies. But it was too late now. Alongside academic exercises, I had enjoyed redesigning typical children's clothes. I'd imagined altering the fabrics, adding accessories, making them look really original.

"Wow! Are you really going to poke your nose into those dusty old things? What a nostalgia fest," Sebastien teased me as he went past.

I shot him a furious look.

"I'm sorry! I was only joking," he said, kissing me on the cheek. "Your drawings are really good. Are you coming to bed?"

"No, not straightaway. I want to look at these a while longer."

I caressed the sheets of paper with my fingertips the way you caress a dream. What if I decided to bring my dream back to life? Would Sebastien understand? Would he support me? I couldn't answer that question . . .

... *sixteen* ...

I confided to Claude my concerns about the way my relationship with Sebastien was evolving. He pointed out how disruptive it could be for my husband to see me calling my life into question in this way. All these changes must be deeply unsettling for him. I had to accept that a transitional period was necessary: after all, I was forcing my little revolution on him; it was not something he had asked for. I had to give him time to get used to it. Besides, any period of change was bound to be accompanied by—for my husband just as much as for me—a whole range of emotions: resistance, the two-steps-forward-three-steps-back feeling . . .

In fact, my concern was twofold: a fear that Sebastien wouldn't follow me as I rethought my professional life, plus a fear that our relationship would keep running out of steam.

"The first thing you need to decide," Claude told me, "is if you still love him."

"Of course I do, even though sometimes I have my doubts."

"Often it's not the other person you no longer love but what the relationship has become. And in a couple you're both equally responsible for what goes on between you. If you want to re-kindle the flame, create sparks! Don't always expect the other person to take the initiative. We've already talked about that."

"So what should I do?"

"Well, one thing would be to work on your 'amorous creativity.'"

"That sounds good! How do I do that?"

"To start with, you could send him a loving text message, but a retro one."

"Retro? What does that mean?"

"Well, now that everyone sends abbreviated, emoji-filled messages, you could try the opposite and send him a proper old-fashioned missive by text—a well-written one, without any spelling mistakes. That would be the height of chic!"

"And besides that?"

"Let your imagination run wild. But there are a few techniques. Identify what your nearest and dearest is most interested in. Then brainstorm with all the words and expressions that come to mind in relation to it. Link together unlikely words, invent expressions to produce an appealing message. It'll be clearer if I give you an example. What's your husband passionate about?"

"He adores Zen Buddhism. He does yoga. And he dreams of us going to India."

"Perfect. Let's make a list of all the words connected to those topics."

With his help, I scribbled on a piece of paper: "Zen. Lotus. Lotus flower. Balance. Breathing, breath. Peace. Beauty. Inner balance. Zen garden. Meditation."

"Make sure you write everything down," Claude insisted. "This is going to be your creative raw material. And remember the ЄQFM rule. Є means no Censorship or Criticism. Q stands for Quantity: you have to come up with a maximum number of ideas. F for Fantasy. Don't forget that! Jot down even the craziest, most improbable ideas. M for Multiplication. One idea can lead to another, linking together like the gears on a car."

"I'll remember that. Thank you, Claude."

"After that, combine the Zen vocabulary with that of love, give it a good shake, and see what comes out, stylewise. You should also think about things like assonance—the repetition of a vowel sound; alliterations—the repetition of a consonant; comparisons; emphasis—heightening the tone; oxymorons—putting two words together that seem to contradict each other, like Shakespeare's famous 'feather of lead, bright smoke, cold fire, sick health'; litotes—which softens a statement, as in 'he's not ugly' to mean he is handsome; and many, many more. But more important than all the lit-crit stuff: follow your heart!"

"It's certainly worth a try."

So I set to immediately, only to realize it wasn't as easy as it seemed. I concentrated hard, pen in midair and searching for inspiration as my eyes roamed beyond the windowpanes.

It took me a good twenty minutes before I felt able to present my "love letter text" to Claude:

My love,

Outside, the skies are overcast and heavy. Inside, the sun shines thanks to the happiness I feel at seeing you again in the haven that is our home. A haven of warmth, of sweetness, a Zen garden that with a kiss becomes transformed into a Garden of Eden. Let me be the lotus flower of your days and the burning wind of Rajasthan at night, to sweep us away to the distant shores of Love's kingdom . . .

Your Camille, who loves you

Claude looked up at me in amazement.

"Heavens, that's impressive for a first attempt! It's excellent, really . . . Of course, writing love letters is only one technique. There are lots of other creative things you could do to get out of your everyday rut. Let your imagination and intuition run free. You'll see that not only will you have fun, but you'll improve your love life as well."

"Are you saying this because you've put it to the test?"

"Who knows?"

ENCOURAGED BY THIS PROMISING start, over the next few days I decided to launch Operation Big Love. I started gently with nothing more than a daily text message. After that, I became more ambitious. I laid traps all around the apartment in the form of romantic Post-its that Sebastien would find between two pillows or when he opened the cookie cabinet.

I didn't exactly achieve the results I was hoping for. In fact, he seemed more surprised than seduced—as if these sudden tokens of affection made him wary. Of course he smiled at me and thanked me with a hug. He even appeared happy, though not overjoyed in the way I had expected. I could tell something was bothering him.

Thinking it over, I told myself he must just be confused. On the one hand, I was doing all I could to get closer to him and rekindle passion between us; on the other, I was freeing myself from my dependence on him more and more every day. My head was full of fresh projects; I was sure of myself and my talents. No longer so needy, the new Camille was flying high! This emotional autonomy ought to have delighted him. Yet he still hung back. His attitude seemed to be "let's wait and see." I was hoping that, sooner rather than later, the change in my attitude toward him—and my amorous advances—would overcome his doubts.

While I was waiting, I continued with the slow, introspective work aimed at discovering the real Camille, the creative, audacious Camille who would be able to set me back on the trail of my dreams. I began to create a portrait of her, an original photomontage: cutting out images from magazines, I stuck my head onto the outline of a beautiful, fashionable woman. I put a portfolio of drawings under her arm, with sketches of baby clothes spilling out of it. Then I cut out all different sorts of letters and made words from them, which I stuck on the style guide for the life of my dreams: words like "confidence," "daring," and "determination"; I drew the words "creativity" and "generosity" on the skirt I was wearing in the image. I added photos of my son and husband on top of cutouts from magazines of people striking hilarious poses. The whole thing was really starting to represent what I wanted to become: lively, creative, ambitious, funny, and, last but not least, generous!

Satisfied with my work, I took a photo of my creation and sent it to Claude. His reply came back instantly:

Magnificent! I can see that your dream is taking shape. Little by little, we'll continue refining it . . . The new Camille is starting to appear. To continue on the path of your transformation, I suggest you join me on Thursday at around 12:30 at number 59 rue Saint-Sulpice in the sixth arrondissement. Good night, and by the way: instead of counting sheep before you fall asleep, tonight try to remember three nice or encouraging things that happened to you today. It's amazing, you'll see!

Claude

... seventeen ...

As I left the Métro, I wondered what kind of surprise Claude had in store for me this time. He had a unique way of staging his lessons, of demonstrating his advice or concepts life-sized. I laughed to myself when I thought of the face I must have made when he wanted to take me up in a hot-air balloon. Just so that I could get rid of—both metaphorically and literally—all the things that were contaminating my mind. And how wonderful it had felt when we were so high above the ground! Another symbol for greater well-being in the future, combined with immediate, concrete gratification. And then the house of mirrors! So what was it going to be today? I was surprised to find myself hurrying when I arrived at rue Saint-Sulpice in order to get to number 59 as quickly as possible, like a little girl impatient to open a present.

I came to a building that was wall-to-wall glass. The front windows were modern and light, the interior a designer's dream. It took me a few moments to realize what this was, and I pushed open the door with a mixture of curiosity and amusement: Claude had brought me to a . . . smile bar! An idea that . . . made me smile! I knew of course that such places existed, but this was the first time I had been in one.

Claude was waiting for me, perched on a high stool, chatting to the female owner like an old friend. They both greeted me warmly. I felt as though I were on a TV makeover show. Claude wanted me to have a "Brilliant Smile" teeth-whitening procedure. I wasn't so sure, but he insisted: he saw this as part of my overall training and progress.

The owner showed us into a small cubicle, and Claude took advantage of the few minutes we had to wait to talk to me.

"Camille, I'm sure you realize that I haven't made you come here simply to have your teeth done."

"I guessed as much. I'm beginning to know you a little."

This made both of us smile. After all, this was the place for it.

"As well as it being important to look after your teeth, I wanted to remind you how important your Smile Capital is. Because your smile can make you far richer than any lottery ticket!"

"Aren't you exaggerating a little?"

Ignoring my remark, he went on: "A smile costs nothing and yet has a huge influence on the people around you, as well as on your own state of mind. So you get a double benefit. You must know what Abbé Pierre said: 'A smile costs less than electricity but gives much light.' It's even been shown that a sincere smile offered to another person can produce a chain reaction that creates up to five hundred smiles in just one day—without taking into account the benefits in your own brain and body. Did you know that a recent study in the States has proved it? Researchers asked a group of volunteers to hold a spatula in their mouths. The ones in the first group had to keep it there without showing any emotion. Those in the second group had to do so making themselves smile. And those in a third group were to smile naturally. Then they submitted them to tests with various levels of stress, such as having to plunge their hands into icy water. For each test, they recorded the variations in their heartbeats. In the group who had to remain expressionless, the rhythm increased considerably. In the group with the forced smile, the results showed a much lower heart rate. But it was slowest among those who were smiling naturally. So what does this experiment show? That the mere fact of smiling, whether naturally or not, reduces the effects of stress on the human body. The scientists are adamant about it. And the explanation? The brain interprets the smile, whether natural or not, as a sign of good humor and sends out calming hormones. Isn't that wonderful?"

"Yes, it is."

"So you see, Camille, smiling not only means others like you more, it lets you be happier and live longer and in better health as well. Not to mention that you're so much more beautiful when you smile. It lights up your whole face, and you look much younger. The next step for you is to learn to release your 'inner smile.'"

"My inner smile?"

"Yes. It's a smile directed at yourself, a smile that brings inner peace—that famous holy grail that often seems inaccessible to us poor Westerners, with our lack of spirituality. It has to be said that we don't really have people anywhere near us who can teach us about it, not even at the university, where they're far too busy giving lectures on marketing or law. In ancient times, the Tao masters taught the art of the inner smile and explained that it guaranteed health, happiness, and a long life, because that smile is like immersing yourself in a bath of love. Not only does the inner smile boost energy, but it also has considerable healing powers."

"Wow! And what do I have to do to develop it?"

"You can train for a few moments every day. Each time you have a few minutes to yourself, sit down quietly, relax all the tension in your body, loosen your jaw by opening your mouth a little. Become aware of your breathing and how this relaxes you physically. Hold on to that breath and think of it as a kind of internal massage. That's when you'll find your inner smile: you'll feel a profound sense of well-being, of release, of calm. Perhaps you could visualize a flower blossoming in your solar plexus."

"To tell you the truth, Claude, I don't know if I'll ever be sufficiently relaxed for that kind of thing. I rush around too much."

"Don't jump to conclusions. Try it a few times. You might be surprised at the result. At first it's hard to stay still—that's completely normal. But as the days go by you'll get real pleasure from being in that state. It's a bit like blue sky. You like the beautiful blue skies by the seaside in summer, don't you?"

"Yes, of course. They're marvelous. But here it's gray the whole year round."

"Well, finding your inner smile is a bit like rediscovering your beautiful patch of blue sky whenever you want to. Even when the sky is overcast, it's just as blue! And when you're in a bad mood, there's this magnificent blue sky waiting inside you. All you have to do is learn how to reconnect to it."

"Great sales pitch. Bravo . . . I'll buy it!"

At that moment, a young woman came into the cubicle. My treatment was about to start. Claude vanished. I let the assistant get to work, dying to see the result. Soon I was able to admire my new smile in the mirror. *Impressive!* The treatment really worked. Delighted, I rejoined Claude, who was back sitting on the stool, talking to someone apparently waiting for a cubicle to come free. He said good-bye to him and came over to me.

"Now you're equipped to give a flashing smile to the whole world, Camille. But remember: it's even more beautiful when it comes from inside."

... *eighteen* ...

That afternoon I experimented with Claude's suggestions in the street. I decided to channel Audrey Hepburn. I tried out my brand-new smile on the men I passed, at the same time attempting to exude the alluring charm of a woman sure of her own worth. In honor of my role model, I made a great effort to combine confidence and elegance.

The results were surprising: four approaches in twenty minutes! The first two gentlemen told me I had a lovely smile. The third invited me for a coffee. The fourth gave me his card and asked if I'd like to go on a date. Needless to say, this did wonders for my self-esteem! I reveled in this proof of my powers of seduction. And I dropped a small positive anchor, to help me on gray days in the future.

At the office, my change of attitude did not go unnoticed either. For fun, I adapted my role model according to the situation. Sometimes I became Steve Jobs, which made me much more confident. At others, I was an athlete like Serena Williams, with a calm strength that could overcome anyone and anything. It became a game for me, and I was amazed at the effect it had on my mind-set and my office life. I was so much more grounded that it seemed to make my colleagues respect me, whereas before I had been the butt of their often sarcastic jibes. The effect was enhanced further because my transformation was accompanied by an unusual enthusiasm for work, which in recent months I had been finding boring, not to say nauseating. This change of course was thanks to more advice from Claude, who recommended that I adopt an attitude of "acting as if": a psychological technique that consisted in *acting as if* this job was the most exciting in the whole wide world. "Get out of it everything that's even the slightest bit interesting. You need to live life at four hundred percent instead of wallowing in your dissatisfaction and hoping that a solution will drop from the skies," he had told me.

For several days I had worked my socks off, smiled right, left, and center, and my boss was among the first to notice.

"Camille, I haven't seen you like this in ages. You're full of energy at the moment, and I like it! Are you sure you don't want to go back to working full-time? Think about it—it could be really good."

I could hardly believe it. I was coming out of my shell and being praised to the heavens at the same time. Not only was I flattered, but I was triumphant. It felt like a kind of revenge against the boss who had been undervaluing me. And yet, was it what I really wanted?

Despite that niggling doubt, my increasingly positive attitude continued to spread through the office. Even Baldy was looking at me differently, and the idea that I had brought him up short after all the smart-ass comments I had had to put up with from him felt really good. But the new Camille did not want to waste time gloating. The new Camille had promised Claude to undertake all the exercises he was proposing, and one of them, as he reminded me in a text, was that I should look beyond appearances: "Everyone deserves a chance. You have to suspend judgment and any preconceptions. I challenge you to approach someone you're not keen on and get to know him or her better . . ."

Really? I had about as much desire to get to know Franck better as I had to shoot myself. When I recalled how often he had given me a hard time, I felt more like keeping my distance forever. But getting to know him better was one of the boxes to tick in my Promises Notebook, and "not kept" was not an option.

So one Thursday morning I took the bull by the horns and went over to his desk.

"Hi, Franck. Do you have any plans for lunch? I thought we might get a bite together—it'd give us time to talk about things."

I could feel a wave of amazement travel round the whole open-plan office. No one wanted to miss this. I saw Franck cast a sideways glance at our colleagues as though to gauge how they thought he should reply. In a wonderful display of solidarity, they all buried their heads in their screens.

"Ah, oh, yes, why not?" he finally managed to stammer.

And so we found ourselves eating lunch together. He had steak tartare, I had salade niçoise. The tables had been turned: he was shifting in his seat, visibly uncomfortable. Whereas normally he always tried to get one over on me and poked fun at me without the slightest qualm, he had now been completely floored by my unexpected gesture. Masks were coming off . . .

I tried to relax the atmosphere by smiling like a good friend and praising him for his talents as a salesman.

"I've never told you this, but I admire your technique. I'm not surprised you're the number one in the team."

This compliment made him blush. I'd never seen him do that before.

"Camille," he replied in a gruff voice, "I haven't always been very kind to you . . . and I'd like to apologize. You know how it is, you want to show off in front of your friends and you get caught in your own trap. I just want to say that I've always thought you were very brave, working such a high-pressured job at the same time as bringing up your son."

Now it was my turn to blush. So our defenses were breached by a shared smile, and the rest of lunch was far more pleasant. Franck was passionate about model aircraft, and his eyes gleamed like a child's when he spoke of making his own miniature planes. He also admitted that sometimes he felt fed up with work as well. He thought he had gone as far as he could but couldn't summon the energy to look for another job. We ended up talking about our families, and to my surprise I learned that he had been divorced the previous year and how hard it had been for him, particularly being separated from his children.

"I'm sorry, I had no idea . . ."

"I haven't told anyone in the office."

It was my turn to see him in a new light, and I felt a bit ashamed that I had judged him so hastily and superficially. His sarcastic comments had probably been a way to shield himself and keep us at a distance, to disguise how raw his emotions were. It just showed how wrong you could be about people when you didn't pay proper attention or take the time to understand them. Now that I had scratched beneath the surface a little, I found that this colleague whom I had always seen as a prickly hedgehog was in fact a sensitive and rather engaging guy.

We left the restaurant satisfied with our conversation.

"It's been good to talk to you," he said simply.

"Yes, I had a good time. Should we do it again?"

"Yes, let's."

He unleashed a broad smile.

This was another thing I saw for the first time that day: Franck's smile.

... *nineteen* ...

I hadn't been so nervous since the oral exam at the end of my degree. I was in Claude's office to take stock of the progress I had made over the last four months. Yes, it had been four months since I started out on what I liked to call my Butterfly Program. I still had the chrysalis stuck to my body, but the metamorphosis was under way, and I already felt like another person. It seemed to me as if I had lived those four months more intensely than all the previous five years! I could feel an incredible renewal of energy and a sharpening of my intellectual focus. Claude would probably explain this phenomenon as resulting from endorphins and other hormones, boosted thanks to positive thinking, smiles, and the feeling of taking charge of my life again.

Claude greeted me warmly.

"How are you?"

"Good, thank you. I think things are moving in the right direction."

"Great. So we're going to assess how far you've achieved your objectives. How does that sound?"

"All right by me."

"Let's start with the things you've done. Have you brought your Promises Notebook?"

"Yes, here it is."

Nervously, I handed him the little spiral notebook. Among the boxes I had ticked: "Smile at ten people at least every day"; "Take greater care of myself and of how I look"; "Choose an image/style that highlights my personality."

"Great progress, Camille! Congratulations."

But there was a box I hadn't ticked: "Lose ten pounds."

"Let's take a look at that."

He pointed to a bathroom scale and waved me to get on it. I swallowed, nervous of the result.

"That's one hundred forty-two pounds. You've lost eleven pounds. Well done, Camille. Now you can tick the box."

I was so proud of myself! I'd finally shed those extra ten pounds.

Claude continued to examine my list.

A box that was ticked: "Do exercises wherever you are."

Another one: "Develop your love life."

"You've put that down as 'ongoing.'"

I cleared my throat and explained: "Yes, I'm trying different things, but Sebastien doesn't yet seem a hundred percent convinced."

"That's only normal. All these changes must seem extraordinary to him. Keep going, I'm sure it'll work."

"We'll see."

"What about the Positive Notebook? Have you been keeping it regularly?"

"Yes, here it is."

Claude leafed through the book where I had written down my recent pleasant memories:

My rose bush has produced a new bloom.

Board game with Adrien, a real bonding moment.

Successful lunch with Franck, my former office
nemesis.

Four men came up to me because they found me
attractive.

Treated the whole family to a delicious home-cooked
meal.

"Camille, I have to say that I'm really proud of you. I think you deserve this . . ."

Opening a drawer, he handed me a pretty little box with a ribbon that I recognized by now. I was so pleased to open it and find a new charm: this time it was a green lotus. I added it to the two others on the chain. Another level! I'd been awarded a green belt in changing my life . . . This was getting serious. I smiled calmly and sensibly—the smile of a person who had matured a lot in a very short time—but inside it felt like Carnival time in Rio! I wanted to run out into the street and hug the passersby. I was as happy as the day Adrien got an A+ on his exams. I could have downed a bottle of bubbly!

Claude brought me back to earth.

"You've made a good start, but there's still a long way to go. I suggest we work for a moment on your next set of objectives. Is that all right?"

I agreed.

An hour later, we read out together the steadily lengthening list:

Continue to adopt positive techniques to increase a
state of Zen and harmony.
Continue to work on relationship with Sebastien.
Set boundaries with Adrien but work toward easing
tension between us.
Clarify the new project for work. Study its feasibility
and the ways to make it happen. Start carrying
it out.

I couldn't help giving a deep sigh. To think that only a few moments earlier I had been jumping for joy . . . Claude saw how discouraged I was and said, "Don't give up, Camille. Remember the saying 'Rome wasn't built in a day.' Keep focused on each task, every mission."

"Thanks, Claude. Really, thank you for everything you're doing for me."

He shook my hand warmly, visibly pleased at my progress. How many people would work so hard to help someone like this with no guarantee of being paid? Frankly, I thought he was crazy, but I had to admire him for it.

... *twenty* ...

I went on doggedly applying Claude's advice, day after day. By now I knew by heart what I needed to do to get myself into the virtuous-circle column. But as he often said, the important thing was not to know but to *do*! He was always praising the benefits of regularity and tenacity.

By the end of the fourth month, I had the impression that I had crossed a critical threshold: I was beginning to really appreciate my new way of living, eating, moving, thinking . . . I was on the brink of reaching the famous mind/body reconciliation the Asian teachings so insist on. The few minutes I spent every day on exercises and stretching had put me back in touch with my body. A body that, somehow, I had not really been living in until now. I ended up enjoying the exercises and even looked forward to how they made me feel.

When I walked in the street, I tried occasionally to imagine my body as a hyphen linking sky and earth, to feel myself as part of a great *totality* rather than as an isolated entity lost in nature. I became aware of just how cut off I had been from my feelings. But from now on I was determined to live in the present. Gone were the days wasted in going over and over the past or in torturing myself about the future. It was so relaxing!

I also began to realize the role that nature and fresh air could play in my physical and mental well-being. Having grown up surrounded by concrete and pollution, I had convinced myself I didn't like nature. But I'd had entirely the wrong impression of it, imagining millions of tiny crawling or flying creatures lying in wait in vast, silent green landscapes that promised the epitome of boredom. Getting in touch with nature again brought me unexpected comfort. I would never have thought I could absorb so much energy from its marvels.

One day Claude decided to introduce me to ikebana, the Japanese floral art that aims to relax and calm the spirit by creating a silent dialogue with nature. We set out for a walk in the country armed with clippers to gather plants. Then, under his watchful eye, I had fun creating a "floral poem" that combined a subtle balance of shapes and colors.

Whereas before I never had time to be still, now I spent several minutes each day in front of the Zen hearth that I had built. Inspired by the Japanese tokonoma, it was an alcove decorated with a kakemono scroll painting, an ikebana floral composition, and several symbolic objects: a candelabra, a statue, a work of art. I had found the perfect spot for it, a small, previously unused corner at the far end of the living room. I placed a long, plain vase on the floor to put my ikebana creations in. On the wall I hung three different-sized cubes. Each of them contained items to inspire and motivate me: the first had a laughing Buddha and next to it a pretty postcard with the inscription "To do what you love is freedom; to love what you do is happiness." The second had a beautiful candle and my three favorite books of the moment. In the third were a family photo of the three of us and a small statue of the venerated Hindu god Shiva, often presented as "the auspicious one." A few soft, brightly colored cushions on the floor encouraged a contemplative break from routine.

Whenever I felt stressed out, I treated myself to a few moments of peace in this corner, staring at the candle flame until I was almost hypnotized by it.

This change in my philosophy of life sustained me from within. As the weeks went by, I felt a great deal less anxious, less agitated. I also became aware that in the past I had tended to focus on my disappointments. No wonder I was chronically out of sorts.

Claude had suggested an antidote to this negativity: to find room every day for a few "moments of gratitude." And so I got up each morning with a "thank you" in my head and went to bed each night with the same thought. Thanks for having a healthy son, having a roof over my head, of living in a country at peace. Thanks for having a companion alongside me to love and support me. I even got into the habit of giving thanks for less important things: a steaming-hot cup of coffee in the early morning, an apple tart shared with my family.

I also took to heart the idea of taking care, every day, of the people and things around me. Taking care of a plant, an animal, of yourself, of your loved ones, but also of everyone you met on your way who might need it. "You only live insofar as you give," Claude had quite rightly said to me once. He had also sent me a book of the Dalai Lama's thoughts to nurture my new mind-set. He had taken care to underline some passages with a marker.

A few phrases in particular stayed with me, such as "By encouraging altruism, love, tenderness, and compassion, one discourages hatred, desire, or pride."

Such ideas had always resonated with me, but in recent years, out of laziness or carelessness, I had let them slip. The secret was never to stop acting on them. To think of them every day. If you don't, you quickly resume the default position of making no effort. And bad habits along with it.

I also liked this quote: "Some people see the mud at the bottom of the pond; others gaze at the lotus flower floating on the surface. The choice is yours."

This seemed to me a good illustration of the different ways people view life. Little by little, I became aware of what makes for happiness: becoming involved—in a loving relationship, a family, work; it didn't really matter what!

As for what gives life meaning, it now seemed to me that it

involved getting to know how to give the best of yourself based on the qualities that made up your true identity. Be good at what you do and be good to others. Wasn't that the key?

Some might object that they are not good at anything. That in fact they are bad at everything. By now I was convinced that such people simply have too many toxins in their mind-set. The good news is that it is perfectly possible to detoxify your mind and reveal your potential for development. Everyone has good qualities. The trick is to identify them, then help them flourish. This will give you the essence of what is best in you.

All this was going through my mind when I received a message from Claude that echoed my own thoughts:

Good morning, Camille! Your tasks for the coming three weeks: positive thinking, autosuggestion, and meditation. You need to practice these every day if you're going to reprogram your mind-set. You're going to be busy! But it's all in a good cause, isn't it?

I sent him a text in return: Why three weeks?

He replied immediately: That's the shortest length of time it takes for change to take root and become a habit.

Together with this he had sent me a small package. I rushed to open it. Within some bubble wrap was a kind of glass jam jar. It looked nice but for some reason made me wary. Inside it, Claude had inserted a scroll of paper. I unscrewed the top and took out the message. It ran for two long pages:

Camille,

Here is your swear-jar . . . It will be a kind of store to prevent wallowing and negative thoughts. You are to put a euro in the jar each time you have a pessimistic idea or say anything unconstructive. I can only hope you don't end up with a fortune in there!

I can't repeat this enough: positive thoughts have a real impact on your body and your psyche. Some very serious studies prove it. Here's one example, an experiment carried out under scientific conditions. They filled two containers about the size of a dessert plate with the same amount of earth. Then they planted twenty-three grass seeds in each of them, with the same amount of compost. They put them in a greenhouse next to each other to make sure they would receive exactly the same amount of sunshine each day and enjoy the same temperatures while the seeds were germinating.

The only difference was as follows: three times a day, each of the researchers took turns to sit in front of both containers. In front of the first, they said very negative things, attacking the seeds verbally: "Nothing will ever grow here, nothing is going to happen, this will never produce grass, I really don't think this soil is fertile. And even if it does grow, I'm sure it's going to wither and die . . ." In front of the second pot, they behaved completely differently: they were confident and said nice things. They were very positive about the seeds germinating and the possibility of seeing grass grow: "I can hardly wait to see these seeds sprout—it's going to be great! The weather is fine, the temperature is perfect, that's going to help as well. I've got green fingers, everything I plant is a success."

Three weeks later, a photo of the two pots appeared in *Time* magazine. I hardly need tell you that from the first pot, which had been exposed to the negative comments, only two or three feeble shoots had sprouted. The second, on the other hand, was covered in a dark green grass, deeply rooted in the soil and already robust and tall. I'm sure you've understood my point, Camille: our words give off vibes. Our attitude as well. If they have such an amazing influence on seeds, just imagine the effect they can produce on people! That's why we have to pay as much attention to our inner dialogue as to our comments to others. Why not make a start today?

Hoping to see you soon,
Claude

I was impressed by the example he had given me and more than ready to try to change. But I sensed how difficult it would be for me, as I had for so long been in the habit of expressing the negative rather than the positive. Claude had warned me: just as the athlete has to train every day, so reprogramming one's thoughts demands tenacity and effort. Not to mention being vigilant all the time, because it's so easy for the mind to slip back into the bad old habits if you're not careful. I promised myself I would be extra vigilant and put the jar on the bookshelves in the living room where I could see it easily. I even decided to see if the men of the family would play the game as well.

Adrien really liked the idea.

The next morning, Sebastien emerged from the bedroom, clearly grumpy after a night without much sleep. He went over to the window.

"God, look at this weather. It's so depressing."

I didn't even need to say anything: Adrien did it for me.

"Dad! One euro!" he cried, delighted to have caught his father out.

Sebastien started to protest but quickly stopped when he realized that the more he grumbled, the more money he would have to put in the jar.

"No, no, no! OK, I won't do it anymore, I don't want to end up completely broke."

And he went over to give his "guardian of the positive" a big hug.

As for me, I tried every day to practice "positive thoughts and attitude." To alter the way I put things. To make them not negative but positive. To make them not passive but active. A real mental somersault!

I had printed out a short fable that Claude had sent me and that I often reread. It's the story of a man who goes looking for a wise man to learn from him.

"Tell me, you who are so wise, what is in your mind?"

"In my mind there are two dogs, one black and one white.

"The black dog is full of hate, anger, and pessimism. The white one is filled with love, generosity, and optimism. They fight all the time."

His disciple is rather taken aback.

"Two dogs? Who fight each other?"

"Yes, almost all the time."

"And which one wins?"

"The one I feed more."

It was clear that for years my thoughts must have been much more like a large Doberman pinscher than a pretty little Maltese puppy. Well, I'd just have to adjust the canine register of my mind. In a manner of speaking.

Claude added another principle to my already long list, one that came from the Emperor Augustus's favorite adage: *Festina lente*, or "Make haste slowly." It seems that like many other people, I habitually confused speed and haste. In recent years I had spent my time doing everything quickly and badly, living like a fly caught in a jar, buzzing around, beating my head against the glass walls of life, and not allowing myself the time to sit back and take stock.

So I urged myself to live life more slowly. To refuse to accept the tyranny of the fast lane. To act, of course, but not to give in to useless pressure. To understand the huge difference between good and bad stress.

I was putting this into practice at work when I received a fresh message from Claude. He was suggesting yet another mystery rendezvous the following Wednesday. At an address in Charenton-le-Pont. All he said was that I should bring a swimsuit and a towel.

A swimsuit? But there was absolutely no way I wanted to go swimming!

... twenty-one ...

That Wednesday I arrived at our meeting place feeling a bit grumpy—although, to be fair, I had put a euro in the swear-jar. Unlike me, Claude seemed on top of the world and excited. What surprise did he have in store for me this time?

It didn't take long to find out. He had brought me not to any ordinary swimming pool but to one that specialized in scuba diving. When I realized this, my heart started pounding. I was trapped: surely he didn't want me to . . .

Yes, he did.

I tried to protest, to get out of it, claiming that I had never learned to hold my breath, that I wasn't sure I could do it for even ten seconds. Claude waved away my fears and told me the point of the exercise: he wanted me to understand the importance of my breathing in channeling my emotions and to stay in control of myself in any given situation.

OK . . . I got the general idea, but did I really have to prove it by trying this extreme sport? As if by magic an instructor appeared with all the equipment, and quicker than I could say "Stop!" I found myself strapped into a load of very heavy gear that I didn't have the faintest idea how to use. My brain almost ceased to function: I found it hard to follow and retain the instructor's directions, especially when it came to the signals for communicating underwater. If Claude thought I was going to play at being a mermaid, he had another think coming! Rather than graceful and agile in the water, I looked more like a hippo brought up in the Sahara. With the regulator stretching my mouth and my hair spreading all round me like tentacles, I looked more like Medusa with her snakes than the sweet Little Mermaid, Ariel.

Be that as it may, the sight of me underwater gave Claude a good laugh. I tried to give him a little kick, but the water slowed all my movements. He must have seen the frown spreading across my face, but he did not relent, apart from asking with a signal if I felt all right. I shrugged to show that I didn't, but the instructor soon led me down to the bottom of the pool and I became completely absorbed in the experience. At first my anxiety made my heart race. I had to force myself to breathe in a controlled fashion to calm myself and avoid hyperventilating. All at once I understood—I could sense—that breathing was the key to managing my movements. After a few unsuccessful attempts I began to judge things better. I even found myself able to float up or down just by controlling my breathing. The sense of weightlessness was exhilarating! By varying the amount of air in your lungs you could control how high you rose, becoming heavier or lighter as you wished. That meant I could adjust my position underwater with minimal effort.

By the end of the session I felt completely at ease and even dared turn a few somersaults by pushing off from the side of the pool. Had I overdone the oxygen? I felt light-headed!

"So, how was it?" Claude asked me outside the changing rooms.

"Wonderful! But you could have warned me." I poked him in the ribs to wipe the sly grin off his face.

"Ow!" he said, laughing. "It would've been a shame to miss it; you looked so charming. A mermaid in a swimming pool!"

I pulled a face.

"If I'd told you what I was up to, would you have come? You wouldn't, would you?"

He was right there.

I left the swimming pool feeling much prouder than when I had gone in. It was a unique experience that would be added to my list of powerful memories and anchors in my Positive Notebook.

While we were waiting for the bus to take us back to Paris, Claude insisted on making another point.

"We should spend a couple of minutes reflecting on the lesson to be drawn from this experience: whenever you find yourself under stress, concentrate on your breathing and remember what it felt like to be diving underwater. How calm it is below the surface, peaceful, the way you managed your breathing, your self-control. You need to become aware of your breathing even on a normal day. Bear in mind that healthy breathing is not merely breathing in but also the way you breathe out. If you expel all the air in your lungs, that gives them the chance to refill with new air, which will help your body more."

"You're right, it's something you need to know."

"And now you do."

... twenty-two ...

With all that I was learning from Claude, I tried hard each day to live more aware of myself, even when I was doing the most mundane things. Brushing my teeth or chewing my food became new and interesting experiences and increased my sensory awareness. I understood the saying "To live in a dream world" much better now. It was true that you could go through life disconnected from yourself, with the annoying consequence that you were never in the only place that really matters: the here and now.

The previous evening, Claude had sent me a text message with a formula I really liked:

Today is a gift. That's why it's called the present.

But the more aware I became, the harder it was to see my family continuing to live in what I now saw as the wrong way.

So that evening at dinner I exploded.

"No, Sebastien! Get off your laptop—we're eating. That's

the flippin' limit! We don't see much of you as it is, and if when we do you're not really here—"

"But I *am* here! I'm sorry, but I'm expecting an urgent e-mail. It's work, so don't get mad up about it."

"In other words, you're not paying any attention to what you're eating."

"Who puts these ideas into your head? That guru of yours?"

Breathe calmly. Don't play the game. Don't get angry . . . Think kind thoughts . . .

"Exactly. I'm working on how to become completely aware, and it's life changing."

"I'd like to see it," he said sarcastically.

"OK, I'll take you at your word. In fact, I was about to propose we do something interesting together in the near future."

"You were? What?"

"You'll see."

I said nothing more: I wanted it to come as a complete surprise.

I was following Claude's method of directly experiencing something that would teach a real lesson. I had found a very special place in Paris that would help me make Sebastien realize, in a concrete, empirical way, what it meant to be fully aware, and its benefits. I was very pleased with myself and was rejoicing in advance at how my surprise would affect him, imagining the amused, sexy look on his face.

However, when the day came and he discovered where I had taken him, he seemed worried rather than pleased.

"So this was your big idea?" he muttered so dubiously that I had a sudden moment of panic. What if this evening, which was meant to be a celebration for just the two of us, turned into a fiasco before it had even begun?

I wasn't having that, so I tried to cheer him up.

"Come on, Seb, trust me. It'll be great, you'll see. It'll be a laugh."

It didn't work. While we were waiting for our allotted attendant, I could see him casting a skeptical glance at the entrance where we were standing, trying to see through the heavy curtains hiding the room where our "festivities" were to take place. The curtains looked like those heavy rubber ones at the start of ghost-train rides at amusement parks.

Our host, Vincent, finally arrived. He instructed me to stand behind Sebastien and place my hands on his shoulders. Then he took Seb's hands and placed them on his shoulders, inviting us to follow him through the curtains.

We entered a room that was in total darkness. And when I say "total," that's still not strong enough. I chuckled, feeling Sebastien's back trembling under my hands. He wasn't exactly enjoying it.

We groped our way until we found our chair backs and sat down for this blind-man's lunch. I have to admit that at the start I didn't feel very comfortable either. Enveloped in this complete blackness, the only way we could get our bearings was to judge how far away the sounds were that we could hear around us, and that made me quite anxious. Was I going to be able to survive two hours like this, with no visual input at all, clinging to the table like a life raft in the darkness?

We began to fill the dark space with disjointed conversation, both of us equally lost in this unusual situation, clumsily attempting to learn this new sensory alphabet. And yet to judge by the lively talk and laughter from the other guests around us, it seemed we would soon get over our awkwardness.

Fortunately, the arrival of the first course helped us relax. Vincent, a nonsighted person, took great care of us and served us a surprising dish. In this unaccustomed universe, we tasted it as much with our fingers as with our palates. We also rediscovered our mouths' ability to distinguish different flavors: it was as though we each had 1,001 taste buds. The fact that we were deprived of sight seemed to enhance our other faculties, and the result was an explosion of sensation.

"Well? Now do you see what it's like to eat while being fully aware of what you're tasting?"

"One point to you."

"Admit that this is a nice surprise, isn't it?"

"I admit it. Good plan."

Our voices and words acquired a new resonance. Not being able to see each other's face and expressions, the rhythms of our breathing and intonation became much more important.

The meal continued with one taste adventure following another, punctuated by different wines, all of them subtle delights that detonated in our mouths as our senses continued to reveal their hidden talents. Ordinarily, we only use less than 10 percent of their potential. Just like our brains . . .

By the end of the meal, I could sense that Sebastien had been won over. He talked enthusiastically about his feelings, tried to define as accurately as possible the nuances of the dishes and wines we were offered and to guess which herbs or spices had seasoned the sauces. This new awareness affected him even more than I had expected; awakening his senses seemed to give him a taste for more.

"Thank you, darling. This has been a wonderful initiation. But aren't you afraid that all this might give me ideas about other equally interesting ways we can become fully aware of what we're sharing?" he said warmly, grabbing hold of my bread roll rather than my hand and then knocking over my wine when he finally made contact.

I laughed.

I knew perfectly well what he was talking about. And personally I had absolutely no objection!

... twenty-three ...

I was pleased with my progress and sensed I was on the right track. Yet that did not stop me from feeling painfully on edge at times. I was in a strange euphoric state that disrupted my sleep and undermined my calm. In other words, I was stressed out. I wasn't going to become a Zen master anytime soon. The changes in my life—so many and so rapid—had set my mind reeling. My nerves were overloaded, and it wouldn't be long before I blew a fuse. I desperately needed to relieve the pressure: I couldn't carry on like this, and so I spoke to Claude about it. He saw this as an excellent opportunity to make me conscious of the benefits of meditation and heart-rate control. Concepts that were utterly alien to an Energizer bunny like me.

"There's nothing I like less than sitting still. It makes me feel useless, as if I'm wasting time. I really think that meditation is a no-no for me."

"That's what you say now, Camille, but it's like all the rest: you'll get there. Only a few weeks ago, the idea of doing ten minutes' exercise a day seemed impossible to you. So did eating in a different way."

"Yes, but this isn't the same: it's not in my nature to be Zen."

"No one is asking you to change your nature. Just to alter a few details in your daily life to achieve greater well-being and calm."

"I don't deny it must be great for those who can do it, but I just can't stay still. I've always been that way."

"Always, never! What if you forgot about those absolutes? Don't you even want to try?"

I agreed, slightly ashamed of protesting so much.

"Don't worry, Camille. You can do it. It's simply a question of adapting. Afterward you won't be able to do without it. Did you know that according to some very serious studies, monks and other experts have better health and a stronger immune system? It's worth giving it a shot, isn't it?"

"Definitely, but at the moment it just seems very hard to organize."

"Just one question: Do you enjoy being so stressed, so tense all the time?"

"No, of course not."

"But it must do something for you if you're so determined to hang on to a way of life that leaves no room at all for calm and introspection."

I could see he was going to leave me without a leg to stand on.

"OK, fine," I said, giving in. "I promise to try."

"I'm sure you can do it," he said with a broad smile. "You'll see, there's no great magic to it. All you have to do is train yourself to find a little calm and silence and to learn to look at what's happening inside you. Make a start, two or three times a day, with a session of deep breathing: six breaths a minute for five minutes. That's the rhythm that slows down your system. You can do it anywhere, even in the Métro."

"I'll believe you . . ."

"Another very interesting exercise is the one I call the 'harmonizer': it combines the principles of controlling your heart rate with positive visualization."

"Isn't that getting a bit complicated?"

"Not at all: the basic principle is the same. At some point in your day you need to create a bubble of tranquility by shutting yourself in a room where you won't be disturbed. Sit down comfortably, with your back straight, and try to breathe calmly. Then place your hand on your heart and breathe, while at the same time visualizing your heart swelling up each time you inhale, and returning to normal size whenever you exhale. Once you are perfectly calm, add a positive visualization: a memory that 'warms your heart.' Then try to relive those emotions and sensations as intensely as possible. Simple, isn't it?"

"What if no image comes to me?"

"I admit that at first it might seem rather difficult. But you should build up an 'inner catalog of positive images and memories.' A mental photo album . . . The more you work at it, the more complete it will become, and you'll be able to access it easily."

"Yes, that's not a bad idea."

"But I think that at this point, what would be most useful would be for you to meet a real master in the art."

"I beg your pardon?"

"Master Wu. I'll take you to him. After your visit everything will be much clearer, you'll see."

We drove for three-quarters of an hour before we reached Master Wu's home. I could hardly wait to meet him. While we sped past a landscape of open fields, I discreetly began to control my breathing and to try some positive visualization.

"Caught you, Camille!" Claude suddenly shouted.

"What?"

Again, that sly little smile of his.

"I've been watching you out of the corner of my eye for a few minutes now, and I can see you've started the training already."

"So . . . ?"

"So nothing! That's great. Carry on . . . don't worry about me."

We finally arrived at our destination. The tires crunched on the gravel of the drive up to the house. Several dogs came out to greet us, muzzles flecked with foam, barking gruffly. The owner of the house called them to heel, and the dogs obeyed her instantly. Doubtless she could have made them take a bite out of our ankles or lick our hands simply by raising her voice or clicking her tongue. I was impressed by her natural self-assurance.

Claude had told her we were coming, and her smile was like a pair of open arms.

"Good afternoon, Claude. How are you?"

"Very well, Jacqueline. How about you? It's really good of you to see us. May I introduce Camille? I've talked to you about her."

Jacqueline was a matronly woman, generously built, with a baby face that made her look cheerful. Frankly, this was not what I had been expecting. I was imagining someone more . . . Asian.

"I'm so pleased to meet you, Camille. So you'd like to meet Master Wu?" she asked, a glint in her eye.

"Er, yes, I would."

"I understand! Lots of people would like to get to know him. Follow me."

We went through a spacious living room with an ancient hearth and exposed beams. The gentle winter sun filtered in through wide bay windows.

"What a lovely room."

"Thank you," said our hostess, apparently delighted at my compliment. "Now, Master Wu is in the courtyard. I'll let you go and find him. I'll be in the kitchen. See you soon . . ."

Claude allowed me to go out first. I was already smiling a warm welcome as my eyes scanned the courtyard. My smile gradually faded: I couldn't see anyone. I was terribly disappointed. Had Master Wu already left?

Seeing how crestfallen I was, Claude insisted, "He's over there."

I still couldn't see anyone.

"There, Camille!" he said, pointing.

I followed the direction of his finger. Comfortably installed on an embroidered cushion, a magnificent Persian cat was stretched out, dozing peacefully. He transmitted a combination of majesty and utter peacefulness. I stopped short, in shock. Then, pulling myself together, I turned toward the practical joker. We drove for three-quarters of an hour for this?

"What on earth are you playing at?" I snapped.

Claude's face showed a mixture of satisfaction and contrition.

"Forgive my little game, Camille. But I couldn't think of a better example than Master Wu to show you what complete relaxation can be. If you think you won't be able to meditate, start by learning to 'be a cat' for a few minutes each day. There's no one like him for being peaceful and calm, completely anchored in the here and now."

I shot him a furious look, which led him to seek refuge in the kitchen alongside Jacqueline.

Left on my own with Master Wu, I watched him simply being for a few moments and was surprised to feel a pleasant sensation of peace slowly invade me. As his tail moved to and fro, he seemed to be composing an invisible treatise on the virtues of slowness. His very own hymn to carpe diem. He didn't even move when I plunged my hand into his warm fur to stroke him.

I realized then that I really shouldn't be angry with Claude for having brought me here. Feeling much more relaxed, I rejoined him and Jacqueline in the kitchen. They were chatting away, enjoying a cup of fresh mint tea, "picked from the garden," as my hostess pointed out. I could tell that Claude was searching my face to see how I was going to react. When he spotted my unspoken thanks he seemed happy.

The afternoon ended on a note of culinary delight: a plum tart that more than made up for the long journey.

... twenty-four ...

From the day I met Master Wu, I enjoyed playing at being a cat as often as possible, to the great pleasure of my nerve ends.

Strangely, the more serene I became, the more I felt my vital energy being replenished. And together with that, I must admit, an increasing libido! In all honesty, I was rather thrown by this. Embarrassed by these renewed impulses, at first I tried to ignore them. I didn't dare mention them to Claude, in case he thought I was going a bit too far . . .

In the end, however, I couldn't bear it anymore and forced myself to talk about it.

"I don't know how to say this but . . . well, for a few days now I've been feeling a kind of renewal of my libido, and I don't know what to make of it. I'd like to know if it has anything to do with our program of change."

Plainly taken aback by my question, Claude cleared his throat but then answered anyway.

"It doesn't really surprise me, Camille. Yes, of course it

goes hand in hand with the changes you're going through: the fact of becoming proactive, of taking your life back into your own hands, of working on your body and your mind. All that helps generate positive energy. Which means that you want to live your life as a woman to the full. And that's good news, isn't it?"

"Yes, but I don't know why. It makes me uneasy. That's why I wanted to talk to you about it."

"Mmm . . . I understand. Perhaps what's upsetting you is discovering a part of yourself that you haven't really explored as yet. Another Camille, as it were. A bolder woman, more in touch with her desires and sensuality."

I blushed. "The thing is, I'm still not entirely sure I like the image that could reflect of me."

"That's only normal. Even today, what we have been taught for thousands of years still influences us deeply. For all those years our sexuality has been constrained by morality and taboos. Such a heritage is bound to leave its mark. And women are only just beginning to enjoy sexual freedom and acknowledge they have desires that are as strong as those men have. Now we just need everyone to accept this new sexual norm."

"You're right. What I'd like to do is to bring some of this new energy into my relationship. To be the one who suggests things, comes up with new ideas, if you see what I mean. Do you think I should take the initiative?"

Claude smiled at me, his eyes twinkling. "Of course. Your husband will be delighted . . ."

I wasn't so certain.

Nevertheless, I did take the initiative. Throughout the whole of the following week I plotted my first surprise. Adrien was left with my mother for the evening. The ever-fashionable little black dress, with a décolletage low enough to make even a long-standing partner take notice. The four-inch heels that I kept for special occasions. Champagne ready to serve in chilled glasses to welcome my nearest and dearest.

A last quick look in the mirror: no doubt about it, I was hot! It had been a long time since I saw myself in such good shape, with sparkling eyes and glowing skin. Sebastien was going to go weak at the knees . . . surely.

When he arrived home, it took him several seconds to get used to the semidarkness before he got a good look at me. Then I gave him my most alluring smile, which brought him up short. I secretly rejoiced at this moment, when I could see from his expression that I had achieved my effect: surprise, bewilderment, interest.

At last!

I decided to go for broke in staging this seduction scene. I played it for all it was worth: a cinematic kiss beneath the spotlights in our living room.

My arms slid round his shoulders.

"Hello, big man," I said.

I was really enjoying seeing how excited, almost intimidated, he was.

"Wow! What a welcome," he murmured. "You're magnificent . . ."

I was bubbling over inside.

"And you haven't seen anything yet," I said, playing my femme fatale role to the hilt.

Our eyelids closed. We kissed again, as if in close-up, gently, passionately.

I pressed my mouth against his, utterly caught up in my own fantasy. My body arched against him, one hand low on his back, the other slipping inside his shirt. I was already imagining the rest of the film projected onto the screen of a night without sleep. I was sliding my hand down his thigh when all of a sudden Sebastien pulled away.

What?

"Are you all right, sweetheart? Is something wrong?" I murmured, my voice thick with the promise of pleasure.

"No, nothing, it's just that—"

At that precise moment my mobile rang. I cursed modern technology. But what could I do? It was my mother.

I had forgotten to put Adrien's antihistamine in his bag. I felt a stab of guilt but tried to reassure her: it was no big deal for just one night. Yes, he could do without it. No, there was no need to go and find a late-night pharmacy. While I was half listening to her, I was casting sideways glances at Sebastien to try to assess his mood.

"Oh ho!" my mother clucked. "From your voice I can tell

I'm disturbing you. So the evening's gotten off to a good start, has it?"

I hated the thought that she was busy trying to imagine what was going on in our apartment.

"Mom!" I protested.

But then I relented. After all, it was thanks to her that I was able to enjoy this quiet evening with my husband. Well, I was hoping it wouldn't be too quiet! So I thanked her profusely before ending the call.

Sebastien had gotten up and was standing by the window with his back to me. I sneaked up on him, took him in my arms, and whispered in his ear, "Hey, what's wrong?"

In order not to have to reply, he rained little kisses on my neck, cheeks, and mouth.

"Sebastien, that's enough," I said softly. "Tell me . . ."

He was avoiding meeting my eyes. I gently took his head in my hands and forced him to look at me.

"I'm sorry, Cam," he said eventually. "I know it's absurd. I don't know what's come over me. There you are, looking stunning, sexy, taking the lead, and all of a sudden, it makes me . . ."

"It makes you what?"

"I don't know . . . It makes me nervous."

I let go of him and took a step back.

"I get it. You don't love me, is that it?"

He didn't say a word.

That hurt. And it made me angry. As disappointed as I was upset, I grabbed the empty champagne glasses to take them back to the kitchen, clacking my heels on the parquet in protest. I made as much noise as possible while I put everything away.

Sebastien had followed me silently and stood behind me. He was as immobile as I was hyperactive, crashing about all over the place. I could sense him gazing at me, a sad, confused expression on his face. After a while I couldn't bear it any longer and confronted him.

"What is it? Tell me. Go on: What's wrong?"

I could see from the way his lips were moving wordlessly that he was unsure how to get it off his chest.

Then all of a sudden he exploded: "I'm stupid, so stupid. I'm sorry. You've changed so much recently, you're so much more . . . whereas I . . . I . . ."

Now he was the one pacing up and down the room, waving his arms around wildly to try to express himself clearly.

He looked so awkward that I felt myself softening. I went up to him and took his head in my hands.

"What about you?" I said gently.

"I . . . I think I'm afraid."

"Afraid?"

"Yes, afraid. All these changes in your life . . . You're forging ahead, changing the way you behave, daring to be yourself."

"So? That's a positive thing, isn't it?"

"Yes . . . it's good, but . . ."

He couldn't spit it out. No doubt he was worried about what I might think.

"But what, Sebastien?"

"What if I don't change quickly enough for you? What if I'm not good enough for the new Camille?"

So *that* was it! It was the last thing I was expecting him to say. I was really touched. I looked him straight in the eye and smiled with all the love that I felt.

"There's no chance of that. I love you, Sebastien, more than ever. And I'm making all these changes for you too, so that you'll always want me."

Again, he said nothing, but this time brought his lips close to mine and stifled my doubts with a long, voluptuous kiss. And this time, no one and nothing interrupted him.

... *twenty-five* ...

From that night on, the atmosphere at home changed completely. A warm wind blew on our love, reviving embers that seemed only too willing to burst into flame. As for my son, I had decided to adopt the principles Claude had suggested: to stop making such a big deal of parenting and taking things too much to heart. In short, to take my daily chores less seriously. "Come down from your cross, we need the wood," Claude had told me one day with a laugh, to help me understand I had to give up my role of a martyred mother on the verge of a nervous breakdown and look at things in a different way.

First and foremost, I took the time to become more interested in Adrien's world. On the sly, I got myself up-to-date with all the latest news from the world of soccer. I even learned by heart the names of the best players and the main rules of the game. So instead of being a dreary waste of time for me, the next match night was a real joy: the astonishment on the faces of my boys was something to behold! For once, Adrien sought my attention as much as his father's: "Did you see that, Mom?" he kept shouting, slapping my back like one of his friends. And when his favorite team scored, it was my arms he jumped into to howl "Goooaaal!" There was no doubt I'd scored a goal or two myself.

I also tried to learn about his musical world by listening to his favorite singers: Bruno Mars, Ariana Grande, Nicki Minaj, Jason Derulo, David Guetta. The first time I joined in singing one of his favorite songs, he was amazed, and I thought I saw something like admiration mingled with respect in his eyes.

My new approach completely altered the tone of our relationship. At last we were beginning to talk to each other again.

Taking advantage of this, I tackled the contentious issue of his homework.

"You know, Adrien, I hate it when I get angry with you. When I have to shout at you about your homework and then we have an argument. It makes me feel dreadful . . . I'd really like things to change, wouldn't you?"

He nodded.

"Do you think you could tell me why you find it so difficult to get down to your work?"

He took his time to think this over, and I was touched that he was trying so hard to explain.

"I don't know. The problems aren't easy, and there are too many of them. And then you get so angry about it that I get angry too. I'm scared I'll mess up and you'll shout. Which means I don't even want to try anymore."

This hit home, and I thought of Claude's advice to lay my tendency to criticize to rest and instead to talk of my own feelings, to say "I."

"When I get upset," I explained to him, "it's because I'm worried for you. I think about your future, and I'm scared that you don't take your studies seriously enough. It's so important for later on that you work hard at school. What I want is for you to have the best possible life when you grow up."

"I know that, Mom. But you worry too much! You don't trust me enough."

"That's possible," I admitted with a smile. "I'm only trying to be a good enough mother."

"Whoa! You're a supermom."

"Do you really think so?"

"Of course," he reassured me, taking my hand in his with an impish smile.

My heart swelled with gratitude. I thought of the positive learning techniques Claude had taught me.

"What do you think about changing the way you do your homework?" I suggested.

"How?"

"Well, we could try to make it more fun, for example."

"That'd be cool."

"Gimme five!"

We high-fived and then had a big hug.

"I love you, Mom," he murmured into the crook of my neck.

I hugged him even tighter.

"And I love you too, sweetheart."

From then on I started to help him with his work in a way that was less orthodox but oh so much more fun. For example I used the principle of Grandmother's Footsteps for the answers to his homework: you can take one step toward the table if you get it right, but go back two if you get it wrong. Or learning lessons through singing. It was a huge success! Not only did Adrien learn three times as quickly, but he also enjoyed himself.

I used the same approach to help with cooking. Instead of making myself hoarse yelling for help that never came, I thought of a trick to motivate Adrien: I convinced him to create an imaginary restaurant with him as head chef. His eagerness to join in and play the game surprised me: I hadn't expected such a positive reaction.

He took the idea so seriously that he even created a completely original recipe for meatballs with seven spices, Indian style. I diced the meat, and he minced it. I cut up garlic, and he made breadcrumbs. Whereas normally it was almost impossible to get him away from his screens, he seemed completely fascinated by this. The final stage of rolling the meatballs in egg and then the breadcrumbs with sesame seeds was a real celebration. I had a flashback to him five years earlier playing with Play-Doh in that magically absorbed way little children have.

During this intense cooking session we didn't say much but smiled and gestured in complete harmony. As a Michelin-starred chef, Adrien enjoyed giving me orders as if I were his assistant, a role I accepted happily because I was so pleased to see my strategy succeed.

These changes also gave me more time and energy to undertake another hugely important task: launching my new professional project. I had made up my mind: I didn't want to carry on with my career in sales but to go back to my first dream—to design and make children's clothes.

As Claude never ceased reminding me, it was time for me to make what I did with my life coincide with who I was and what I believed.

I began by making exploratory inquiries. In my heart of hearts, I didn't want to take on a franchise; I wanted to create my own brand, my own concept. I quickly had to face facts, however: the market for off-the-rack children's clothes seemed saturated, and there were very few openings.

Another unavoidable conclusion: with the economic crisis, people would never spend huge sums on baby clothes that would be too small only a month later.

So what could I do?

Inspiration came when I did some "googlestorming," something Claude had mentioned as a good way to come up with ideas.

I came across a Dutch company that proposed a kind of "fashion leasing": you rented a pair of jeans for a year, just like a car or an apartment. By paying a five-euro monthly subscription, clients could be sure they always had a brand-name article of clothing that was trendy too, while at the same time promoting sustainable fashion and in the end being able either to buy the article or to return it and rent something else.

My brain kicked into gear: Why not use the same principle for baby clothes? Ethical garments for children from birth to three years old. I could give them added value by making each one unique in design and fabric. I would only need to link up with manufacturers of basic sustainable clothing—rompers, T-shirts, pants—and then customize them. Fashionable ready-made clothes to suit every budget. I felt like I was onto something.

My mind was racing, carried away by my enthusiasm. All parents love to create a "look" for their child. Who hasn't drooled over adorable, tiny baby clothes? The only snag: the prohibitive price of items that are outgrown so quickly. But with my idea, proud parents would be able to renew the wardrobe of their little darlings by leasing rather than buying it! I did a quick calculation and confirmed that a five-euro monthly subscription could work.

I enthusiastically set to work on the details of my project. I began to create my first basic designs to have something to show my future partners.

On Claude's advice I approached a business incubator—a company that helped entrepreneurs develop new ideas—and prepared a thorough business plan to present to them. After that, I crossed my fingers in the hope that the company's accreditation committee would accept my proposal.

Things were looking decidedly rosy. I could feel the good

vibes. Two weeks later, when I received a positive response from the start-up people, I almost collapsed in gratitude. And in spite of what were after all reasonable doubts, Sebastien had decided to support me. Now all that remained was to announce the "good news" to my mother. That thought was much less enticing. To her, having a staff position was the only possible way to work. Knowing her as if I had brought her into the world—rather than the reverse—I was very apprehensive about telling her. And I was right to be.

... twenty-six ...

When I rang the doorbell to the little apartment where I was raised, my mother greeted me with a broad smile and a big hug. I was apprehensive about what I was about to tell her. I knew that in a few moments our harmony might be dashed to pieces.

"Sit down, darling, I'll be with you straightaway. I just have to see how supper's doing. It's veal stew . . ."

"Mom! You didn't need to go to so much trouble. I said we could just have something simple."

"It's absolutely no trouble, and I love making it."

I gave in. As ever.

I sat down on the sofa in the small living room, legs crossed and my anxious heart keeping time with the big art deco clock that dominated the room, brought back from a visit to New York.

My mother came to join me, delighted at the idea of a girly chat.

"There we are! Now I'm all yours."

When I cleared my throat, she noticed how uneasy I was and a shadow flitted across her face.

"Are you all right, darling? You look—out of sorts?"

"The thing is . . . I've got some important news for you."

"Oh my god. Are you leaving Sebastien?"

"No, Mom . . ."

"So he's leaving you?"

"Mother," I hissed, annoyed. "Why do you always have to project *your* anxieties onto *me*?"

Her face grew darker still.

"I'm not projecting, darling. I'm just being realistic about life. Just look at what your father did to us."

"But that's what happened to *you,* Mom. It doesn't mean things have to be the same for me."

"You're right, I'm sorry. So what is this important news of yours? Oh, I know! You're pregnant."

And why did she have to keep going on about that? Couldn't she accept the fact that I didn't want another child?

"No? OK, so tell me what it is," she said, taking hold of my hand.

"I'm going to quit my job."

She snatched her hand away.

"You're not, are you?"

"Yes, Mom. You see, some time ago I met an incredible man—"

"You're cheating on Sebastien!" she said indignantly.

"Mother! Stop interrupting and let me explain. Of course

I'm not cheating on Sebastien. The man I met has been counseling me over the past few months to help me take stock of my life and try to recapture the happiness I had lost."

"What do you mean, lost? I thought you *were* happy. Why didn't you tell me? I don't understand . . . You have a job, a husband who loves you, a wonderful son . . ."

"Yes, Mom, I have all that and I thought I was happy too. But then one morning I woke up feeling completely empty but terribly restless at the same time. Thanks to Claude, I'm finding a meaning to life again."

"Claude? His name is Claude? And what does he do?"

"He's a . . . routinologist."

Silence.

"It's a new approach to personal development. It's very effective," I said, trying to justify myself.

"It sounds like nonsense," she immediately retorted. "You know you have to be careful . . . there are so many charlatans about these days. They say they'll make your dreams come true and give you a better life, but once you're hooked . . ."

I knew she'd say that.

"Mother, it's not like that at all. When will you stop treating me like a little girl! You don't have to be frightened for me. I know what I'm doing."

Another silence, which set my nerves jangling.

"I'm finally going to fulfill my dream, Mom. To start working in children's fashion."

"You do realize that it's a pretty crowded area, don't you?"

I could tell she was veering between anxiety and anger.

"Yes, but I've come up with a unique concept. Do you know what leasing is?"

"Leasing? No . . ."

"It's a practical, economical, and sustainable system that allows people to rent things, with the possibility of buying them later on. It's already very common with car dealerships and toy makers. In the current financial crisis, parents don't want to buy luxury clothes for their babies. It's too expensive when they only use them for such a short period of time. But I'll give them a chance to rent them, paying only between five and fifteen euros a month. I'm sure it'll be a huge success!"

I was getting carried away, but it was obvious that my mother didn't share my enthusiasm.

"And that's what you're giving up a permanent job for? When all your life I've tried to make you understand how important financial stability is . . . Do you realize you could destabilize your family if it doesn't work out? What'll happen to Adrien if you run out of money?"

"Why must you always imagine the worst? I need you to believe in me, Mom! Not have you shooting down all my ideas. You're always so pessimistic."

"What does Sebastien think of this?"

"He's supporting me. We've done the math to make sure we can get by in the early days."

"But it's such a risk . . ."

"Yes, but isn't life itself a risk? You have to understand that to me this project is a huge breath of fresh air. I feel as if I'm living again, as if I'm finally being *me*."

No response. It was like pissing in the wind.

"OK, I think I'll go now. I can see you're not going to accept this."

She didn't try to stop me. It was as though she'd been hit with a sledgehammer.

Out in the street, a wave of conflicting emotions swept over me. I was sad that my mother didn't understand me. Annoyed that she never trusted my ability to make a go of something, and yet at the same time liberated because I had had the courage of my convictions. I had been true to my dreams and to the real me. And at last I had stopped trying to please her. I was daring to live my own life and not one that my mother had imagined for me. Despite this, I was still a little uncomfortable in this new skin of mine. I was excited about my new project, but what would happen if in the end I failed? What if my mother was right? These thoughts niggled away at my happiness. I had to talk to Claude about it: Surely he would be able to help?

... twenty-seven ...

Claude had arranged to see me for another of his unpredictable but enlightening lessons. This time, though, I knew exactly where we were to meet: the Louvre. I couldn't figure out why he had dragged me here, and as we made our way through the interminable galleries I wondered what on earth he would pull out of his magician's hat this time. While waiting to discover this, I told him about my confrontation with my mother. He seemed distant somehow, which wasn't like him at all. He must have something on his mind. Was he actually listening to me? I was doing my best to explain how I was feeling and how badly my mother's skepticism had shaken me, but he didn't react at all, just carried on strolling past the paintings.

"Claude, you're not listening to me!" I finally protested, annoyed. How could he be so detached when I was in such turmoil? After all, he was the one who had brought me here! If it was just to see him acting as though I wasn't there, what was the point?

He did not reply but raised a finger to his lips to stop me talking. This made me so furious I almost exploded. However, he sped up, and with an enigmatic smile well suited to this temple to the *Mona Lisa,* he led me to the room with all the works of the great master Leonardo da Vinci. Still without a word, he made me sit down on one of the benches in front of his last great masterpiece: *The Virgin and Child with Saint Anne.* We stayed for a long while gazing at the canvas.

"What can you see, Camille?" he eventually asked me.

Perplexed, my eyes surveyed the painting in search of its meaning.

"Well, I can see the Virgin Mary, who seems to want to pick up the baby Jesus, but at the same time the child is trying to get away from her because he's more interested in grabbing the ears of that lamb. As for Mary's mother, Saint Anne, she looks to me to be rather detached, but she has a kindly face."

Claude smiled at my description.

"In fact, Camille, I brought you here to show you this painting and to explain that for me it reflects the mother-child relationship."

The mother-child relationship. An image of Adrien whispering into the crook of my neck, "I love you, Mom," flashed through my mind, while at the same time I could almost feel the warmth of his body against mine. Then I saw myself in my mother's living room again, trying to explain to her my ambitions for a new career while she constantly interrupted me.

"The lamb symbolizes sacrifice," Claude continued, "and

the fact that Jesus takes it in his arms means that he is accepting his own tragic destiny. His mother, Mary, is trying to protect him from the suffering to come. That's why she is reaching for him. As for Saint Anne, she is watching without getting involved, which shows that symbolically she accepts her grandson's fate."

This explanation of what for me only a few moments earlier had been nothing more than a charming pastoral scene took my breath away. Hanging on Claude's every word, I gazed at the painting with renewed interest, waiting impatiently for what he would say next.

"Every mother is afraid for her child and tries to keep him from suffering, Camille. It's natural. It's intrinsic to motherly love. But sometimes that fear can hold the child back. He has to fulfill his destiny and make his own way in life. Until now, you have constantly been trying to win your mother's approval. You have stifled your own wishes to keep her happy and not let her down. It's as though all this time you've been walking in shoes that pinched. And now that you're announcing that you want to follow your own path, it terrifies her. That's only normal. But you have to learn to let her be afraid, not to take it on yourself, and to follow your own destiny. Have faith in yourself. Once she sees you flourishing and happy, she will be happy too, believe me."

"I hope so, Claude. I really hope so."

As I said this, I wondered exactly what kind of mother I was to Adrien. Was I doing things the right way? Was I letting him flourish to the best of his ability? He was still young, and his wishes and needs were those of a child . . . but what about when he grew up? When he had to make his own choices, to find his way as a man? Would I be able to let him do so without projecting onto him expectations that were not his, just as my mother had done with me? Would I know how to really listen to him and help him fulfill himself? We think we're acting for the best, but sometimes our fears and even our love can blind us.

Claude had fallen silent, as if to allow me time to think. I smiled briefly to show that I was all ears once more, and he went on: "Today, Camille, your mother is afraid that this change of direction you're embarked upon will hurt you. But she is going to have to understand that at some point *not* doing anything is what would really hurt. The worst thing is not failure. It's not having tried. And besides, you can never protect yourself against future suffering, because that's part of life. It's impossible to escape it. Life is made up of the rough and the smooth. Everyone has to accept that as being an integral part of life's rich tapestry. Resisting it only reinforces our dissatisfaction. That's why wise men learn to act on the things they can control, not on those they can't. You can't change external events, but you can change the way you react to them."

His words seemed to me like a trickle of cool water on a hot summer's day. They strengthened my determination to press on in the new direction I had found for myself and gave me a lot to think about for the future, when I myself would be faced with my son forging his way as an adult.

So when a large group of noisy foreign tourists burst into the gallery and interrupted our absorbing conversation, I could not help tutting disparagingly.

Claude himself remained impassive, a broad smile on his face. Did he never get annoyed? He led me into another room, still giving me advice: "Camille, can you see how you allow external factors to impact you? You're letting them control your sense of well-being. If that continues, you'll never really be on top of things, and you run the risk of being forever tossed about like a little cork on the waves. On the surface, a wise person may seem to be navigating a storm, but deep down, everything is calm. The secret is to regain control over your mind-set and decide that you will make the most of even unpleasant things. To see the positive even in the negative. You'll see: if you approach life like that, it alters everything."

"All right, but even so, it's not that easy to control your thoughts. We don't always react rationally. I certainly don't. For several days now I've been having doubts, I'm no longer sure of anything about my project . . . I'm scared. It seems so risky! And it's not just my mother who has reservations. My best friend and my uncle have also told me they think it was mad to take on something so uncertain in the middle of an economic crisis. I'm wondering whether I shouldn't put the brakes on it all."

Laying his hand on my forearm, Claude talked to me in a warm, reassuring voice as if I were a little girl scared of the dark.

"Camille, what if to begin with, you replaced 'I'm scared' with 'I'm excited'? It's a trick that often works well. Oscar Wilde used to say, 'Wisdom is to have dreams big enough not to lose sight when we pursue them.' You're the one who is right to take a leap of faith. Let me tell you a story. I think you'll find it soothing. And it should boost your confidence.

"Once a year, in the frog kingdom, a race was organized. Every year there was a different goal. This particular year, they had to get to the top of an old tower. All the frogs from the pond gathered to watch the event. The starting gun was fired. When they saw how high the tower was, the frogs in the crowd thought the competitors would never be able to reach the summit. They started saying things like:

"'Impossible! They'll never make it.'

"'Frogs can't climb up something like that!'

"'They'll dehydrate before they get up there.'

"The competitors could hear them, and one after another they began to feel discouraged. Only a few went on climbing. The onlookers kept insisting: 'It's not worth it! None of them can make it. Look, they've nearly all given up!'

"The few remaining frogs admitted defeat, all except one, who simply went on climbing despite everything. And, alone, after a supreme effort, the frog reached the top of the tower.

"Stupefied, the others wanted to know how he had done it. One went over to ask what his secret was, only to discover that the winner . . . was deaf!

"So be careful, Camille, not to let yourself be influenced by the opinions of those around you. Don't get discouraged. Even those who love you sometimes project their fears and doubts onto you. Take a good look at the people bringing you down and make sure they don't contaminate you with their negativity."

Claude's words echoed in my ears for a long time and did their job. I couldn't and, above all, didn't want to turn back: I was too attached to my new career, and I knew how important it was for me to see it through. It was a question of integrity. So I symbolically put on blinkers and inserted earplugs, determined to keep pushing forward.

... *twenty-eight* ...

My good-bye party at the agency filled me with a mixture of joy at the thought of freedom and anxiety at my uncertain future. Had I really made the right choice? I'd surprised everyone. Most of my colleagues just took me for a mother, pleasant enough, happy to glide along in a cozy rut, and yet here I was transformed into a daring entrepreneur!

The meeting room was pretty crowded; my boss had invited the other sales teams as well. He wanted to take advantage of my leaving to build up links between the different sections. Two birds with one stone.

Some of them were completely indifferent to the fact that I was going, and to me personally: they had just come to munch on peanuts and drink the free champagne and didn't even say hello to me. Others, however, did come up to say something, most of them finding it hard to conceal a stab of envy.

"You're setting up a business at a time like this? I've got a friend who did that: he hasn't been able to pay himself anything these last five years. It's not a job; it's charity work!"

"An entrepreneur? Mmm . . . you're going to have to learn to live on next to nothing."

And after these words of encouragement, they invariably left with a "good luck" that sounded a bit like "good riddance."

Their comments made me furious. Why did they have to bring everything back to money? That really got to me. Even on a minimum wage, a dream is still a dream! I had never felt as alive as I did now, and that was priceless.

Happily, a few of my colleagues were really great. Above all, Melissa, the receptionist, who had given me a lovely bouquet of flowers. And Baldy had taken the trouble to buy me a present on behalf of the whole team: a crystal shamrock I could use as a paperweight. It was a magnificent Lalique piece, and I was amazed.

"It's to bring you good luck in all your projects," he explained. "You'll be sure to put it in your boutique, won't you?"

I gave him a big kiss. I was bowled over to see such consideration from someone like him.

My boss also came up to me, and I thought I detected in his eyes a hint of admiration and jealousy.

"All the best, Camille. I really hope your business succeeds. You're very brave to undertake such a venture, especially nowadays when hardly anyone is taking risks! But if things don't work out, don't hesitate to come and see me. There'll always be a place for you here."

"Thanks so much. I won't forget that."

Even if I was hoping never to have to take a step backward.

My desk was soon cleared. Ten years of work in one small box. I felt as if I were in the midst of a dream. It was impossible to tell whether it was a good one or a bad one.

As I walked down the streets toward home carrying my little bundle of leaving presents, I felt strange, detached, reeling from a cocktail of contradictory emotions: relief, joy, a feeling of freedom but also of stage fright, fear, anxiety, vertigo . . .

Over the following days I redoubled my efforts to fine-tune my business plan. I had worked out how much capital I had to put up personally . . . it was meant to be at least 30 percent of the overall total. Even if I emptied all my savings, I did not have quite enough. Would it be sufficient, though, to convince a bank to give me extra funding?

With the help of the incubator people, I prepared a cast-iron dossier. At least, that was what I hoped. With my business plan sorted, I set off to take the banks by storm.

On the morning of my first interview, my stomach was churning. I consulted the time every thirty-six seconds. Finally the moment came. And when you've got to go, you've got to go . . . Besides, I had no nails left to chew.

I had downloaded a playlist of "power songs." After all, there was a reason why armies marched off to war singing.

I listened to Radiohead's "No Surprises" over and over. It's a song that would encourage anyone to forge her own destiny. I walked down the street convinced I was completely different from anyone else, wrapping myself up in a Technicolor movie of my success story. Was what I was feeling obvious from my face? I tried to read the answer on the faces of people I passed; they probably just wondered who the weirdo was staring at them. But what did I care?

My hands were moist, but I could feel wings sprouting between my shoulders: I was ready to fly.

Unfortunately, my enthusiasm did not last long.

The bank manager received me coldly. Hardly glanced at my portfolio. Raised his eyebrows at the shortfall in my own capital contribution and cut short our interview, which lasted barely ten minutes, promising me a swift reply. In that respect at least he kept his word. Forty-eight hours later, I received the thumbs-down.

MY NEXT MEETING HAD the sad air of déjà vu about it. This time, the impact of another bank's refusal caught me in the street, just as I was going home loaded down with shopping. As well as being upset, I was bitterly frustrated. Yet again. I could see my dream disappearing. Fear and disappointment pricked my throat, eyes, and nose.

When Adrien opened the door for me, I barely greeted him. I headed straight for the kitchen so that he wouldn't see the dismay on my face. I was forgetting that children have skilled antennae: they sense everything.

"Are you OK, Mom? Should I help you put the shopping away?"

"That all right, sweetheart, I'll sort it out," I said, pretending to be busy with the cupboards. I was deliberately turning my back to him so that he wouldn't see the tears welling up.

No chance.

"Mom, are you crying?" he asked, leaning over to get a good look at my eyes to confirm his suspicion.

"No, I'm fine, I told you! Why don't you go and play in your room?"

"I'm not leaving until you tell me what's wrong."

Heavens, he was self-assured. Adrien sometimes liked to play at being the man of the house and to patronize me. Sensing he wouldn't give up until I explained what the problem was, I told him about the bank rejecting my proposal.

"You see, I still need a bit of money to launch my new business, and the bank didn't want to lend it to me. That's why I'm upset. But don't worry, I'm not finished yet!"

I tried to smile through my tears, so as not to worry him still further.

He took me in his arms to give me a big hug and said in the reassuring voice of a man of the world, "Don't worry, Mom, it'll all work out."

With that he turned on his heel and went to play in his room. I smiled. What a marvel he was!

After putting away the shopping, I washed up and then started to clean the stove, which I hadn't been able to face the previous evening. I scrubbed away, full of the energy of despair, hoping that this simple chore would calm me down.

As I was setting the table and calling to Adrien to give me a hand, he came into the room with a delighted but conspiratorial expression on his face.

"Mom, here—take this."

He handed me a brown paper envelope.

"Open it!" he encouraged me.

I did as I was told and inside found a bundle of banknotes and at least fifty coins.

"It's for you," he said, beaming with pride. "I've counted it all: it comes to one hundred and twenty-three euros and forty-five cents. And if that's not enough, I'll sell my Nintendo. That way you'll have enough for your business, won't you, Mom?"

I was choked with emotion. My goodness, how I loved him at that moment. And how handsome he was, with his bright eyes and natural enthusiasm, wanting to save me from failure.

I took him in my arms and gave him a big hug.

"Thank you, my love, that's really sweet of you. But keep your money for now. I promise that if I need it, I'll come and ask."

"Promise?"

"Yes, I promise," I assured him.

He seemed pleased and at the same time relieved to be able to keep his savings. Seeing I had a smile back on my face, he must have thought he had been successful and went off blithely to stash his money in his room.

His generosity restored my spirits. There was no way I was

going to give in: I had to keep going for my own sake, for my son's, and for everyone else who believed in me.

It was in this mood that I set off again to seek financial backing and presented my portfolio to a third bank.

Once again, several days went by, and I waited, my morale ballooning with the helium of hope. Hope that once more was popped in midflight.

This third rejection hit me *hard*.

Three banks, and not one of them wanted to finance me. Nothing I tried had worked. Neither my best Audrey Hepburn smile, nor my wise, confident Gandhi air, nor playing the tycoon like Michael Douglas in *Wall Street*.

I succumbed to despair. To anguish as well. I had quit my job, spent money on creating my own designs. If no bank was willing to back me, I was done for. I would have to crawl back to my former boss, beg him to give me a job again, and consider myself lucky to be able to return to my cozy, humdrum little life.

No, I would never do that.

At that point I grew angry with Claude. In fact I was seething: it was his fault I had embarked on this crazy plan! He was the one who had encouraged me to take this step. And now I was going to fall flat on my face. Sebastien would never forgive me. This damn venture could well cost me my husband and destroy my family. Seb would leave me, taking Adrien with him. I'd be ruined, depressed—I'd end up homeless! I couldn't stop my overheated brain from conjuring up disaster after disaster. I was heading for a plane crash.

My mother was right, it's sheer madness! I'll never do it.

Galvanized by a potent mix of fury and fear, I rushed to Claude's office. Him and his stupid method . . . I'd tell him a thing or two! Make him face up to his responsibilities, force him to . . . to . . . I didn't yet know to what, but force him anyway.

I stormed past the secretary without stopping.

"Madame, you can't—"

As if I cared!

I flung open the door to his office. Claude interrupted his phone conversation when he saw me burst in.

"Madame, please . . . ," the secretary tried to insist.

"Don't worry, Marianne. I'll deal with this. Just a moment, Camille."

With that, he calmly finished his phone conversation. His unruffled attitude only annoyed me more: How could he be so calm when I was so upset? Why did he always appear in control when I was such a mess?

"Well then, Camille, what's wrong?"

"What do you mean, what's wrong? It's a complete disaster! I was turned down by a third bank today. I can't take any more."

I was seething.

"Calm down, Camille. There's always a solution."

"Oh, no! Stop right there—I've had it up to here with your positive attitude. Look where that's gotten me! Yes, you and

181

your crap advice! Am I being rude? Good! I believed you; I trusted you. I left my job, and just look at me now, without a cent. I'll be on the streets soon! Tell me the truth: What on earth made you think I had it in me to start my own business? It was obviously going to be disaster!"

Claude let me get everything off my chest without saying a word. He seemed distressed to see me in this state. Hearing my tirade, his assistant knocked at the door.

"Is everything all right, Monsieur Dupontel?"

"Yes, everything is fine, Marianne."

"Madame Theveniaud is getting impatient. You had an appointment with her at half past."

"Could you apologize and ask if she can come back next week? Thank you, Marianne."

So he was canceling another appointment because of me? Given the state I was in, I was pleased I had upset his day. He had pushed me to take risks and throw myself into a completely crazy business venture, and I reckoned he was at least partly responsible if I was going to fail.

"Now, I would like you to calm down, Camille. Three rejections don't mean all is lost. One bank, two banks, ten banks . . . You have to persevere. And if that isn't the right opening, you need to explore others."

"Persevere, persevere! That's a good one. You're not the person who has to look at her family every day and see how worried and disappointed they are!"

"'In the confrontation between the stream and the rock, the

stream always wins, not through strength but by perseverance.' That's H. Jackson Brown Jr.—"

"You know what, your endless list of quotations is beginning to get on my nerves! They're not going to help me get a bank loan!"

"Maybe not. But nor is getting into a state like this. What time is it?"

"What? It's a quarter past six, why?"

"Perfect, we've just got time."

"Time for what now, Claude?" I asked. His endless mysteries were driving me mad.

"You'll see. Come on, get your coat."

"But . . ."

Before I had time to say anything else, Claude had taken me by the arm and rushed me out of the room. There was no stopping him. In addition to his Jaguar (things must be going really well for him), he had a scooter parked outside his office. He put a stop to any more protests by plonking a big helmet on my head.

We sped off through Paris. I clung to him, both exhilarated and scared stiff. The streets rushing past, the anonymous faces blurred by our speed, the blaring horns, the imposing monuments topped by glittering gold, the impenetrable depths of the Seine and its picturesque banks, the Japanese couples posing for endless photos, the street sellers, the curious onlookers, the people bouncing by as if on springs . . . the Paris merry-go-round left me dizzy.

The scooter suddenly came to a halt as Claude parked on a sidewalk, and I snapped out of this urban reverie.

In front of me I saw a big gray stone building: the Church of Saint-Julien-le-Pauvre.

"We're just in time," Claude declared, obviously pleased with himself.

"Claude, really, I'm not in the mood—"

He didn't let me finish but tugged me inside the church and found us two places in the third row.

"Shhh. Be quiet now, and listen."

I reluctantly complied, because a woman was already coming onto the stage, followed by a man in a dark suit who installed himself ceremoniously at the piano.

It took only two songs, with their rich, soaring melodies and subtle accompaniment, to calm me down.

But it was the third song that overwhelmed me. The crystalline purity of the singer's "Ave Maria" floated out over the aisle and gave me goose bumps. Tears welled in my eyes. That such fervent emotion and devotion could be contained within a few notes . . .

Claude kept glancing sideways at me, doubtless overjoyed that the magic was working.

Shivers of delight ran down my spine. I felt as if I was connected to some higher force without being able to say exactly what it was. Despite this, the sensation filled me with strength and vigor.

I sat through the rest of the concert on cloud nine.

At the end, we decided to go and have a drink at the Caveau des Oubliettes.

"Claude, I'm sorry for the way I behaved earlier. It wasn't fair of me. You're doing all you can to help me, I know . . . And if I fail, it won't be your fault."

"'Success consists of going from failure to failure without loss of enthusiasm,' as Winston Churchill used to say."

"There you go again with your quotations."

"Whoops, sorry! I simply wanted to tell you again that what you're experiencing at the moment is not failure. It's part of the hazards and pitfalls of a successful business start-up. I brought you to the church this evening to show you how strong a fervent belief can be. You must keep faith. Above all, in yourself. I believe in you!"

"Mmm . . . ," I muttered, still wary.

"So, you'll try again?" he asked, extending his hand.

I hesitated a couple of seconds, then held out mine as well.

"I'll try again."

A few days later, I succeeded in getting an appointment with Populis Bank. I had read in a magazine that they had a reputation for supporting small businesses that had been turned down by traditional financial channels. This time I didn't let myself get my hopes up. That way I wouldn't be disappointed.

When a week later I was told on the phone that my proposal had been accepted, I could hardly believe it. I waited until I had hung up before I let out a shriek of joy that would have scared the spots off a leopard. I was an inch away from pulling my T-shirt over my face and running round the room like a mad-woman, howling, "Gooooaaaaal!!!"

At last I had been given my passport to a new life.

... twenty-nine ...

This success earned me a fourth lotus charm, this time a purple one. I put it on my necklace and stroked it constantly, like a good-luck talisman. I hadn't dared to hope I could attain all these levels of change, but I had to admit that the method had worked. Now that I had the necessary funds, I could finally set about launching my concept of leasing haute couture baby clothes at accessible prices. I planned to open my boutique in six months' time. And in the run-up to the opening I wouldn't have a day to spare. Sometimes, I felt I had become a bionic, multitasking robot. I had to be everywhere at once: coming up with ideas, bringing them to fruition, sorting out the logistics.

I was going to have to look for help. I needed a second pair of hands. As it turned out I allowed myself the luxury of taking on four: four pairs of incomparable hands that I found among young fashion designers who—I was so flattered—saw that my project could be a springboard for their own careers. They therefore agreed to join me for very little pay until my business was properly launched, betting it would be a success. We set ourselves up in a boutique I had rented on rue Le Goff, a stone's throw from the Luxembourg Palace. It wasn't huge, but it was big enough to start with, and it had loads of charm. Exposed beams, a mezzanine, a very airy back room, and even a basement that could be used for changing rooms and a kitchenette.

I took Adrien to visit.

"It's really cool, Mom!"

What he really wanted to know was if I was going to get rich. He listed all the things we would be able to buy if I did. He could already see himself in the most beautiful cars: a red Porsche one day, black Bugatti the next . . . He was so sweet, his eyes gleaming with excitement, and his joy made me joyful too. Thank god it would be years before he had to knuckle down and take on adult responsibilities.

Dream, my boy, dream, I said to myself. *And may reality forever be kind to you!*

I had also moved heaven and earth to find partners who would supply at a reasonable cost the basic garments made of organic cotton and hemp, as well as others made of alpaca, yak wool, and bamboo.

When I finally received my orders, I stroked these unbelievable fabrics, reveling in the thought of what I was going to make out of them.

During this period, I was filled with unbelievable creative energy. I didn't get much sleep and yet strangely enough felt no ill effects. This astonished me: usually I was like a sedated snail if I missed even an hour of sleep. It was as if I were on drugs. And in a certain sense I was: high on enthusiasm! Bringing to fruition the thing that I wanted most in life was more satisfying than anything I had ever done. I had never known such incredible energy.

... *thirty* ...

Claude followed my progress like a father hen. Speaking of fathers, he often reminded me that on the list of objectives I still had to tick off was sorting out my relationship with my father.

I protested.

"Claude, it's really not the time to ask me to do that. You can see I'm completely overwhelmed. I don't have even a minute to myself."

"On the contrary, there's no better time, Camille. And besides, you know it's been niggling at you for years, like a stone in your shoe. Why put up with the pain another day? You'll be so relieved to have taken a step toward reconciliation. The new Camille doesn't leave problems hanging, does she?"

"All right, all right . . . I'll see if I can find a minute."

I was annoyed that he was insisting I do this right now. But was he really insisting? Deep down inside, I knew he was right. I couldn't let the situation drag on. I had to confront it. I had swept that particular problem under the carpet of my conscience, thinking it would, in the end, be forgotten. Some hope! Over all those years it had never stopped gnawing away at me. Guilt and resentment were all mixed up inside me and undermining my confidence. But how could I forgive the person who left my mother and me before I had even taken my first steps? He wasn't a father; he was just a . . . a sperm donor.

I hadn't seen my father in six years, ever since a terrible scene when I had tried to settle scores with him. On that occasion I really did try to mow him down with a Kalashnikov of reproaches. I had sprayed him with angry bullets without giving him the slightest chance to defend himself. I couldn't have been more bitter if I had swallowed poison. I was determined to hurt him. A little girl's anger can knock over tables and break chairs. All the negative feelings stored away for years had surfaced, erupting like a volcano. I wanted to make him *pay* for his absence. Why had he left my mother? Where had he been when I was frightened, when I was ill, when I needed a father?

Unfortunately, my settling of scores had blown up in my face like a grenade and resulted in an outcome I had not really wished for: a complete break.

Weeks, months, and years had gone by without my daring to take the first steps toward reconciliation. I was afraid of how he would react and, even worse, of being rejected once again. With hindsight, I had begun to understand more clearly why he had left home. I was an accident that happened to him when he was far too young. At twenty-three, he wasn't mature enough to cope with a child, nor did he really want to. Nonetheless, he had helped my mother as far as he could afford to and came to see me from time to time. Those rare, precious moments had left a lasting impression on me, a memory like the sweet taste of cotton candy.

It took me a while to unearth my telephone address book, hidden under a pile of dusty papers stuffed at the back of a closet.

His number was in it.

I sat for several long minutes beside the telephone, heart beating fast, hands moist, mouth dry at the thought of not knowing what to say. Finally I plucked up my courage.

It rang several times before he picked up.

"Hello?"

Silence.

"Hello? Dad?"

Silence again . . .

"FORGIVENESS DOES NOT CHANGE the past, but it does enlarge the future," Paul Boese said. How true! After my phone call to my father, I felt much lighter. It was as though I had cut the rope dragging a line of heavy barrels along in the wake of my boat, holding it back. At first our conversation was stilted, strangulated, struggling to emerge. Soon, though, we discovered the sincere, honest voice of our hearts, and our words somehow built a bridge between us. We agreed to have lunch together. We replaced the silences and question marks of our past history with a new dialogue.

I could scarcely believe it.

... *thirty-one* ...

Oddly, ever since I had reconciled with my father, I had also begun to feel more relaxed about my marriage. Perhaps I was becoming aware of how much, over the years, I had conflated my father's behavior with that of my husband? How far had my relationship with Sebastien been soured by my fear of being abandoned like my mother? But now that was over and done with. Never again would I allow the past to interfere with the present or affect my relationships.

Of course, I couldn't stop my husband leaving me for some-one else, if that was what fate decided. But now I was much more serene about it: I knew that whatever happened I could count on my inner resources to cope. And that certainty gave me a strength I never thought I had.

So it seemed I had made my peace with the males of the species.

One morning I was enjoying this thought, drinking a nice

cup of green tea, when Sebastien came into the kitchen and handed me an envelope.

"Here, there was a letter for you."

Inside was a brief message:

Rendezvous on Thursday at Espace Mille et Cent Ciels,
for a summit meeting! Be on time: exactly half past one.
See you Thursday, Claude.

What was he up to now?

Sebastien, who had buttered a slice of bread, was staring at me out of the corner of his eye as he ate it.

"More work?"

"Er . . . yes. Sorry, nothing I can do about it!"

"You never stop."

I sensed he was worried or ill at ease—I couldn't exactly tell which—and went over to give him a kiss.

"Don't fret; it'll be worth it. And you'll soon see how wonderful it's all going to be!"

"I guess so . . ."

On Thursday I abandoned my assistants in the workshop with instructions for the afternoon and rushed to my rendezvous in a glamorous outfit that won me some wolf whistles and compliments in the street. I blushed, but the meeting place was in the smartest area in town, so I had told myself I needed to fit in. And wasn't it also a perfect occasion to see how I was getting on in the skin of the new Camille? If I was to believe the flattering looks I received, it was going quite well.

As I entered the Espace Mille et Cent Ciels, the sight took my breath away. The lobby itself was like a hymn to the beauty of Asian palaces. Rich fabrics, elegant furniture, subtle fragrances, beguiling colors. I felt as though I had been transported in time and place. It was glorious. And the chandeliers, the antique lamps, the soft, thick carpets, laid on parquet floors or handmade mosaics. I was captivated at once by the seductive semidarkness that threw mysterious shadows onto everyone's faces.

But the greatest mystery remained: Why had Claude invited me here? That was the question I was asking myself when I went up to the receptionist.

"Where's the bar, please? I'm supposed to be meeting someone."

"At the end of the corridor, immediately on the left."

I followed her directions, my heart beating loudly. What was the elaborate setup for this time?

The bar was as magnificently decorated as the lobby. I studied all the people there. None of them looked like Claude. I silently cursed him for being late: I've always hated having to hang around in a place like this. Men are quick to misinterpret what a single woman might be doing there. I tried hard to adopt a distant, self-assured look, repeating over and over in my head a mantra that had become a habit in recent weeks: *I am Audrey Hepburn, I am Audrey Hepburn . . .*

My neighbor at the bar had his back turned to me, offering me a good view of his navy blue suit—which, it has to be said, was very well tailored. *Nice pair of shoulders,* I said to myself before realizing to my horror that the back was turning toward me.

"What are you doing here?" said the man with a disarming smile.

"But . . . but . . . what's . . . ?"

"Well, as you see, it's not only your Claude who can spring surprises!"

Sebastien took my face in his hands as if it were a precious sculpture and gave me a languorous kiss. I was instantly aroused, although slightly embarrassed by how indiscreet and incongruous such a kiss was in a place like this. Luckily, the barman pretended to be looking elsewhere. Sebastien pulled back and stared into my face to judge how I was feeling about his surprise. I had not seen such passion in his eyes for a long time. Too long.

I stammered, "In-incredible! How did you manage to—"

"Shhh. It turns out that your Claude is much cooler than I thought. He was perfectly happy to help me organize this little piece of theater. He wrote that message to make you think it was him you were meeting . . . Fun, wasn't it?"

"Wait till he hears what I have to say about that!" I said, but I was far too pleased with the result to bear Claude a grudge. "Well then, what do you intend to do with me to make up for tearing me away from several hours of precious work?"

"Mmm . . . Things that will make you glad you came! Besides, a few moments of relaxation will only make you that much more productive, won't they, my favorite businesswoman?"

He had come up with a tough schedule. Hammam, sauna, pool, a gentle scrub with black eucalyptus soap. We lay side by side and surrendered ourselves to the expert hands of young Balinese masseuses, whose expertise took us somewhere close to seventh heaven. I relaxed completely, all the while holding on to Sebastien's hand, which only added to the sensuality of the experience. By the time we left the spa, I was floating on air.

The candlelit dinner that followed was the climax of our day together and sent my taste buds straight to nirvana. This place indulged the senses like nowhere else. But what enchanted me most was to discover that Sebastien was gazing at me in the way he used to do: I was his Scheherazade.

And that was more than an objective ticked off. It was a dream come true.

... *thirty-two* ...

That idyllic interlude with Sebastien did indeed give me renewed energy. Luckily, because the period that followed was
terribly stressful. I had to put up with infuriating delays, bar-
gain with grasping suppliers, manage a still inexperienced team,
deal with unbelievable amounts of admin, be creative at night
but supremely organized by day. In short, I was on the verge of
losing it. Fortunately, I had an extraordinary support network.
Family and friends came to my workshop to offer loud, sincere
encouragement. It warmed my heart. I so wanted them to be
proud of me!

Claude, my dear Claude, did not let me down either: he had
promised to get in touch with his media contacts, assuring me
he knew lots of people. That was one thing at least I wouldn't
have to do . . . How was I ever going to thank him?

For now, my baby was becoming ever more lively. The de-
livery date was fast approaching, which meant it was time to

find a name for him. I organized a brainstorming session in the back room of the boutique. Claude had advised me to invite people from a variety of backgrounds to enrich the session—we'd get differing and interesting ideas. So in addition to my team, I asked my hairdresser and my masseuse, who kindly agreed to take part. I told them all about the essential rule for any creative effort: the CQFM. No criticism or censorship; a great quantity of ideas; some fantasy; and ideas that multiplied, one linking to the next. We also had to keep in mind these key points: our target was children from birth to three, and we offered ethical haute couture at off-the-rack prices thanks to our leasing model.

To get our brains working we began by writing down as quickly as possible on a piece of paper all the words that came into our minds. Next we decided to explore more closely the specific vocabulary of early childhood: "Tiny tot, beansprout, stork, pooh-pooh"—we agreed no censorship!—"knee-high to a grasshopper, abracadabra, pat-a-cake, little minx, kitty-cat bambino, peekaboo, pirouette, sweet pea, cradle, this little piggy . . ."

We also wrote down words connected to the worlds of clothes and fashion—"a stitch in time, bluebonnets, nimble fingers, better by design"—and other phrases from nursery rhymes: "Three little kittens, they lost their mittens . . ."

Claude helped us do a positioning map. On the diagram two lines intersected to make four quadrants: the practical world of children; the world of the "enchanted" child; ethical, fair-trade

200

clothing; and fashion for hire. This helped us sort our suggestions, which would make our choice easier.

Then we began the roll call of names.

"'Fashionimo,'" suggested my hairdresser. "Words that end in 'imo' are good, aren't they? There's Nemo, Geronimo, or Pinocchio . . . Or how about 'Minimode'?"

"Good! I'll put that up."

"Why not 'Little Goldfingers'?" said Geraldine, one of my seamstresses.

"Or 'Stitches in Time'?" cried Lucie, clearly delighted with her bright idea.

"What about 'Fortune's Child'?" said Fabienne. "It'd remind people of Destiny's Child. But I guess they're not trendy anymore?"

"'Biomode,'" was my masseuse's idea.

"No! It sounds too medical."

"We said we wouldn't criticize, remember?"

"'The Bee's Knees'?"

"Great, but it already exists."

"Oh . . ."

After we eliminated names already taken, ones that were too long, others that didn't sound right, and those that were too complicated, we were left with a list of four possibilities: Cuddleeco, Green Bambino, FashionFairies, and Li'l Trousso. They all contained a message and said something about the project.

"Cuddleeco" . . . the name suggested both an embrace

between mother and baby and also hinted at our ecological ambitions.

"Green Bambino" highlighted our ethical ideas too, and with "bambino" intimated that we were producing children's clothes.

"FashionFairies" evoked the alluring world of magic, which we thought would attract people buying baby clothes. The fact that it included the word "fashion" was important as well, because the clothes we created were meant to be stylish.

"Li'l Trousso." The notion of "trousseau" implied something that was being passed on. A trousseau used to be a precious collection built up over the years, so we felt this name would lend my concept gravitas by suggesting to the parents that they were giving their child something valuable and unique.

The debate raged for a further two hours. Then a decision was made: it would be FashionFairies. We'd done it! Thank god. We could relax at last.

"Champagne!" I declared, almost euphoric with relief and delight.

I had put a bottle in the fridge in anticipation. While we toasted our success together, I wrote the name in big letters on the whiteboard. My imagination was already working overtime to create a logo for my business.

... *thirty-three* ...

And then . . . and then, the great day arrived. The grand opening, at last!

The boutique was crammed with people. All the guests crowded around me, glasses of champagne in hand. My little fashion empire was decked out for the occasion: a buffet with an elegant snow-white tablecloth, a butler wearing equally elegant white gloves and the obligatory solemn countenance, and a glamorous receptionist.

My mother was clucking around me admiringly. Next to her, my father, who had made the journey especially, couldn't hide his emotion and kept giving me highly indiscreet winks and congratulatory thumbs-up. To see my parents side by side, having buried the hatchet and chatting like a pair of old friends, filled my heart with gladness. Sebastien and Adrien were in the front row, miming vigorous applause and making me laugh. My son had told all his schoolmates that his mother was going to open a high-fashion boutique for children and that she was going to become famous. Naïve, perhaps, yet I was touched by his childish enthusiasm. But what touched me still more was the look of pride on his face.

My sole disappointment was that Claude had not yet appeared. He was going to miss my speech, in which of course I had decided to offer him my heartfelt thanks. What could he be up to? It wasn't like him to be late, and I was worried. So it was with a slightly heavy heart that I began speaking and thanked all those who had played a part in the fulfillment of my dream.

All of a sudden there was a commotion at the entrance to the boutique, and the guests inside turned to look. A fresh crowd of people came in. My heart began racing as I couldn't see exactly what was going on. Cameras started flashing; people were calling out . . . Then, just like the Red Sea in the Bible, gradually the waves of people parted in front of me, making way for . . . Could it be? Jean Paul Gaultier himself! And right behind him, a beaming Claude, apparently as pleased as I was and clearly delighted that his surprise had been so successful.

I was overcome.

My project had already brought me moments of huge satisfaction. When, for example, the printer had called me to announce that my advertising leaflets and business cards were ready. And when the painters put the finishing touches to the magic words "FashionFairies" on my shop front. I had been so moved, so overjoyed I had had to wipe away a few discreet tears. It had been such a long journey in such a few short months!

Would success be my reward? I was counting on this opening evening to give me some idea, but now . . . Now it had surpassed anything I could have imagined. Jean Paul Gaultier. In person! In *my* boutique.

I extended a trembling hand to my hero. He shook it warmly. As if through an enchanted mist, I heard him explain to everyone that he was pleased and proud to sponsor my boutique because the concept had really appealed to him. When Claude had sent him details of the project, he had instantly offered to support it in the media, in order to give FashionFairies greater visibility.

"Camille has a great talent as a designer," he went on. "Her baby clothes are truly original. And to offer families the opportunity to get top-of-the-line garments at low prices by leasing them is incredibly clever. Bravo, Camille!"

I couldn't believe my eyes or ears. This was Jean Paul Gaultier, and he was saying these amazing things about me! I could feel tears welling as he concluded: "I will be pleased to offer her my support and, if she wishes, my advice!"

Bliss.

The reporters took photographs of the two of us together. They bombarded me with questions for their articles. Thanks to Claude's tremendous efforts, my concept was going to be in all the papers. This was more than a helping hand; it was a trampoline!

As the evening was drawing to a close, Claude came up to me. I grabbed him for a hug. I owed him so much!

"Claude, I don't know how to thank you for all you've done for me."

"I'm delighted at your success, Camille, and I'm very proud of you. I think you deserve this . . ."

He held out to me the famous little box, this time wrapped in a golden ribbon. I could guess at once what it contained: the black lotus. The last of my talismans.

My eyes filling with tears all over again, I kissed him and added the charm to the ones I had already received.

"I have to go now," he said. "Once again, my congratulations!"

Before leaving, he slipped a small white envelope into the palm of my hand. I opened it after he had gone.

The paper inside read:

My dear Camille,

Please allow me to arrange one final meeting with you. I have a few things to tell you, and then my mission with you will be complete. You will be able to continue on your way in the knowledge that you are on the RIGHT path. Meet me the day after tomorrow at 2 p.m. on top of the Arc de Triomphe. Bravo once again, and good night from your devoted Claude.

What surprise did he have in store for me this time?

... *thirty-four* ...

So I was to meet him on the top of the Arc de Triomphe. By now I knew Claude and his love of metaphors: what better place for this rendezvous to mark the end of his mission with me? There was no doubting that his "teaching" had been a triumph. But, given his modesty and the care he had taken to emphasize my progress and accomplishments rather than his success as a mentor, I suspected he wanted to celebrate *my* triumph, which was visible both in so many small ways in my daily life and in much bigger things, of which FashionFairies was the prime example.

I walked up to the monument, admiring the impressive sculptures, allegories of victory, adorning its arches. Yes, really, what better place to celebrate the successful conclusion of my personal project and to pay homage to the brilliant counseling that Claude had offered. Head held high, my eyes glinting with pride, I passed by the Tomb of the Unknown Soldier and felt a similar flame burn inside me.

When I reached the top of the arch, I looked down at life

going on beneath me. All those tiny dots rushing in every direction, the cars the size of toys, passersby like colored pixels. The wind was ruffling my hair, and I breathed deeply, inhaling the air of freedom and ambition that seemed to envelop this place so redolent of history and conquest.

Claude was already there and welcomed me with open arms.

"Claude! I'm so pleased to see you!"

"Me too, Camille. So, have you recovered from the other night?"

"Oh yes. It was marvelous! Thank you again for all you have done. And to bring Jean Paul Gaultier along with you, that was miraculous! I still don't know how you managed to pull it off."

"Ah, that's my little secret . . . But you know, if your concept hadn't appealed to him, he wouldn't have come. So the credit is all yours. Have you seen all the plaques on this monument, Camille? Magnificent, aren't they? I couldn't think of a better spot to round off this mission. All these symbols of victory, liberty, peace. That's what you've achieved—thanks to your own efforts, your strength of will, and all the positive changes you've brought about in your life."

"I would never have done it without you."

"Everyone needs a guide sometimes, and I'm pleased to have been able to help you . . ."

Both of us fell silent for a moment, staring at the extraordinary panorama we could see from the top of the arch.

"You know, Camille, I like to think we are all citizens of the world, but few people are aware of it. Anyone could become a peace ambassador simply by working on his or her own inner serenity and happiness. Just imagine the impact if more and more people chose the virtuous circle rather than the vicious one . . ."

"That's true, and it's why I'm so pleased I'm back in the 'good' circle. You've taught me so much. Even if your mission on my behalf is over, I sincerely hope we'll continue to see each other."

Silence.

"Claude?"

His face had suddenly clouded over.

"Maybe when you've heard what I have to say you won't want to see me again."

"What are you talking about?"

"I have to tell you a secret that might destroy your faith in me."

"Now you're frightening me."

"OK, so here goes . . ."

I stared at him, willing him to go on.

"I am not a routinologist."

I was dumbstruck. *What?*

"In real life, I'm an architect. I designed the house you stumbled into the day of the storm. I'd always dreamed of being a great architect. But fifteen years ago, I was lost; a fat, depressed, middle-aged guy with no future. In those days I lived in the United States. I was a waiter in a pizzeria, light-years away from achieving my dreams. I put on forty-five pounds. I ate because I had been hurt, and the wound had not healed . . . All because of a love story that ended badly."

Claude was struggling to speak, and I could tell from his face how painful that episode must have been for him. He went on: "I had left France after a disastrous breakup with the woman I thought was the love of my life. It was brutal. She went off with my best friend . . . Their betrayal almost destroyed me. We were about to start the third year of our architecture degree and were planning to get married when we finished. But there was no way I could stay after what happened. I felt I had to get as far away as possible, to abandon everything, including my professional future, and forget her. To put an ocean between us was the least I could do. But when I got to the States, my depression only got worse. I completely let myself go. I was huge."

A memory suddenly clicked in my brain. I exclaimed: "So that man in the photo was you!"

It was his turn to not understand. I had to explain how I'd found the photo in the drawer in his study.

"Yes, that was me all right. The other man is Jack Miller. He's the one who looked after me and set me back on track so that I could become what I am today. Without him, I would never have returned to architecture: I no longer had any confidence in myself. He was my mentor, my . . . routinologist."

"What do you mean, *your* routinologist?"

The wind tousled his salt-and-pepper hair. His eyes shone. He sighed deeply, then clearly decided to tell me everything.

"Camille, the moment has come for me to explain. Routinology as such is an invention. In reality it's a kind of mutual aid chain, a way of passing on success: whoever has been helped becomes a routinologist in turn and has to choose another person to help and pass on everything he or she has learned."

"But . . . but . . . that's not possible. It's . . . It can't be true!"

"But it is."

"What about your office? Your assistant? And that young woman who said she had been counseled by you?"

"All that was staged. In fact, that office is my architectural practice, and Marianne is my assistant there. I had to take her into my confidence and convince her to play along. The woman who agreed to say she was a former client is in fact my great-niece. The only other things I had to do whenever you came were to remove anything that could give away my real profession and leave out a few fake routinology files . . ."

"So that was why there was a design for a house with the calculations and a heap of papers?"

He nodded silently, watching me to see how I would react.

"That means you really have no qualifications to be my life coach? No track record?"

He coughed. This was the first time I had ever seen him lose his composure.

"Yes and no, Camille. You see, each new 'routinologist' has, like you, been through an apprenticeship that he then follows scrupulously. It worked for you, didn't it?"

I sensed that he was waiting for some sort of absolution from me. I wasn't yet completely ready to give it. I was going to have to digest all this first.

He must have read my mind, because he went on: "You mustn't think I don't know what you're feeling, Camille. It was a shock for me as well to learn that Jack Miller wasn't a routinologist . . . It's true that it isn't a classic method, or even an orthodox one, but it's worth it, don't you think?"

We stared at each other. An intense silence hung in the air while he waited for my answer.

I capitulated.

"Yes, it's worth it."

Claude breathed again. Smiling, he rummaged in his bag and pulled something out.

"In that case, you're ready to have this."

He handed me a thick notebook. In it I discovered all the stages of my program, the exercises, the learning tasks, the detailed instructions. I was deeply moved to see page after page covered with notes, diagrams, photos. What an impressive collection.

"I've been keeping it for you throughout your journey. It will be very useful later on in helping the man or woman you choose to mentor. And by the way, it will only take a look or a word for you to know who that person is . . ."

"Is that what happened in my case?"

"Yes. I'd been waiting for four years to find someone I wanted to mentor like this."

I was stunned and flattered at the same time.

He gave me a box of routinologist business cards printed in my name (as if he had never doubted I would agree) and some bogus files, photos, and letters of thanks that I was supposed to pin to the wall of my future consulting room . . . the whole paraphernalia of being a routinologist.

"Here you are. Take them, please. It's your turn to pass on all you have learned. You will do that, won't you? You won't allow the chain of routinologists to break?"

There was a pleading note to his voice.

I was stunned. He was still staring at me insistently. My mind was filled with all that we had been through together. I was choking with emotion. I held out my hand and took the papers . . . I owed him that at least, didn't I?

... *thirty-five* ...

The raindrops crashing against my windshield grew larger and larger. The wipers creaked and shuddered, yet I was totally calm, despite the rain, the mist, the gridlocked traffic, and the red pool of light that the taillights spread through the night. For the first time in my life, I felt completely at peace, "aligned" as Claude would have said. Gone were the days when life tossed me about like a leaf caught in a violent storm. I was continually amazed at my own inner resources. I felt I was connected to a force whose existence I had not even suspected until now. I felt ready to confront whatever life threw at me. At last I had learned to take hold of the reins of my life, and I was never going to let them go.

Around me, stuck at the traffic lights in their metal boxes, all I could see were gloomy, angry, weary faces. I felt like winding down my windows and shouting Claude's instructions on how to be happy at the top of my voice. Instead, I made do with smiling blissfully while I waited for the lights to change.

Green! I accelerated away, keen to get the traffic moving. Just then a vehicle jumped the red light and smashed into me . . .

Blackout.

Soon afterward, the sound of sirens.

Oh, what a handsome fireman, I told myself as I was being lifted from my car.

He took me over to the fire engine and sat me down to recover from the shock. A few moments later, a woman flung open the door: the woman who'd crashed into me. She began to babble apologies at me, crying, groveling, saying how stupid she had been, how useless she was, how hopeless . . .

I listened without interrupting. There was no point in me saying anything even if I had wanted to: when it all has to come out, it all has to come out. Neither of us was hurt, apart from a few bruises and scratches. More of a fright than any injury. In spite of this, she could not forgive herself for having caused the accident.

Once we had given statements to the police and dealt with the rest of the formalities, we moved our cars to the side of the road to free the route. Our insurance companies would take them away soon enough.

To recover from the cold and shock, I suggested to my still-apologizing road-rammer that we go for a hot chocolate while waiting for the tow trucks. She seemed both grateful and incredulous that I should be so kind to her.

Now she could not thank me enough. I didn't mind the

verbal avalanche: the poor woman really seemed at the end of her tether.

We ordered our hot chocolates—Viennese for me because I needed the comfort of that little dollop of Chantilly. I could see the woman's lower lip start to tremble, and I sensed she was on the brink of confiding in me things she had bottled up for far too long.

I laid my hand on her forearm to encourage her.

"Don't worry," I said. "It's not that serious. Besides, my insurers are getting to know me. I used them only a few months ago. Seeing how much we pay them, it's just as well they have something to do."

Tears began to well in the corners of her large, distressed eyes.

"Than . . . thank you! You . . . you're so kind! In your place I think I would have gone berserk."

"That wouldn't have done much good."

"I'm so . . . so . . . sorry! I don't know what's happening to me lately. Nothing is going right. My nerves are in tatters, I feel like chucking it all in . . . and now this. Today has been just . . . appalling. It's too much."

She broke down in a torrent of sobs. This started me thinking . . .

My heart began to race. Had the moment come? *She's the one,* I thought, feeling quite emotional myself.

Would I be up to it? Unconsciously, I sat up straighter in the bistro armchair and took a deep breath before I plunged my hand into my coat pocket and began to stroke the little piece of card I found there.

"What's your name?" I asked her.

"Isabelle."

I held out my card.

"Here, Isabelle. Take this. The thing is, I might be able to help you . . ."

She snatched my business card with the incredulous expression of someone who found it hard to believe anyone could do anything for her.

"I'm a routinologist."

"A routine-what?"

Pocket Dictionary of
Routinology Words and Phrases

Act as If: The mental technique of "acting as if" consists in behaving *as if* the situation bothering you or the thing you have to do that least appeals to you were the most exciting activity in the world. Live it 400 percent, rather than drifting along: do not sit around waiting for change to drop into your lap.

Amorous Creativity: Dare to be creative! Brainstorm loving ideas, and jot down all of them following the principle of CQFM. C: no Censorship or Criticism. Q for Quantity: produce the maximum amount of ideas. F for Fantasy: note down even the most ridiculous and improbable suggestions. M for Multiplication: one idea leads you to think of another. Whether you write inventive "love letter texts" or find unusual places to meet to surprise your loved one, creative thinking will always be your greatest ally in the battle against routine.

Art of Modeling Yourself: This involves finding role models among celebrities or fictional characters, people whom you admire for a certain quality or aspect of their lives. Like Camille, you can list them ("I'd like to have the wisdom of a Gandhi, the calm of a Buddha," etc.) and make a collage of their photos and hang it somewhere where you will see it regularly. Or you can imagine that you are such and such a person and act accordingly so as to gain self-confidence. Choose the best from your mentors—attitudes, behavior, philosophy—and construct your own template for success.

Be a Cat: You can "be a cat" by allowing yourself a moment that is entirely yours, a peaceful, calm moment anchored in the here and now. You will be able to stretch, yawn, let your ideas float like a soft meditation. Being a cat is simply to be happy "being," without the pressure of "doing."

Deep Breathing: Two or three times a day, make time to do some deep breathing. Sit down, relax your body, loosen your jaws by opening your mouth slightly. Breathe in for a count of four, hold your breath for two, breathe out for four, hold it for two. You will gradually increase your breathing capacity and will be able to breathe at a rate of eight (breathe for eight, hold for four), twelve (breathe for twelve, hold for six), or sixteen (breathe for sixteen, hold for eight).

Note: Exhaling is all-important, because the more completely you breathe out, the more you fill your lungs with new air. This supply of oxygen will refresh your entire body, not to mention your brain.

Dramatic Triangle: This is a principle that describes the three symbolic roles we play in turn, more or less consciously, in a negative relationship: that of victim, persecutor, or savior. There's never a good way to resolve this triangle, apart from quitting the game.

Elastic Bands: The "elastic bands" of the past are events that have affected you but that you do not realize are still influencing you in the present. Situations in your current life can re-open those wounds and in spite of yourself release an emotional charge out of proportion to the event unleashing them. In order to live the present more fully, you need to identify these elastic bands and to cut them, first by recognizing their existence, then by doing something about them—for example, working on repressed anger from the past or incomplete mourning either through writing therapy or by seeing a counselor.

Empathy, Wet and Dry: "Wet" empathy is when you take on board another person's problems and absorb their negative emotions. This will only lead to you feeling bad as well. "Dry" empathy is when you listen at a distance, so you can understand and sympathize with the problems of those around you, but you are not contaminated by all the negative vibes. It is a useful shield to protect yourself.

Feeding Your Rats: You "feed your rats" if you encourage that part of you that likes to complain and play the victim. What you need to do is stop feeding them and become aware of how this negativity nurtures fear and opens up secret wounds. This will make you less vulnerable, because you are surer of yourself.

FEET: When you find yourself in a tense or hurtful situation, rather than reach for your "reproach machine gun," express your grievances clearly and calmly. To do that, remind your interlocutor of the Facts that upset you. Then express your Emotion, how this made you feel. Encourage the other person by suggesting a way out. Then propose a Truce by pointing out how things could improve, creating a win-win situation for both sides.

Imaginary Camera: To use your "imaginary camera" and modify your "perception filter," you must go in search of Beauty, focus your attention on pleasant and joyful things in the street, on public transport, wherever you go. This will help you build up a catalog of positive inner images that will be really helpful in reprogramming your brain to be more positive also.

Inner Catalog of Positive Images and Memories: This goes hand in hand with your imaginary camera. You create a mental photo album of pleasant, peaceful moments that you can recall regularly to rediscover those "good vibes." This reinforces a healthy mind-set and a positive view of the world.

Inner Dialogue: To change your "inner dialogue" for the better, there is a proven technique: every morning in front of the mirror, repeat positive statements about yourself. Even if you do not yet entirely believe them, your brain will hear and register them. This will boost well-being and help restore a positive self-image.

Inner Smile: The masters of Tao taught the art of the "inner smile"—or the art of regaining inner harmony—a guarantee of health, happiness, and longevity. This is a state of well-being created by regular relaxation and deep-breathing exercises. The inner smile also encompasses the capacity to accept others, to show them—and yourself—sympathy, generosity, and love. Once you attain this state of mind you will attain—in the familiar term—"inner peace."

List of Positive Experiences and Good Qualities: Draw up a list of the major experiences in your past that illustrate your successes, your good qualities and capabilities. This will let you focus on the positive areas of your life or personality, and so help your self-esteem.

Mission Spring-Clean: This involves cleaning *inside* and *out.* *Cleaning inside means* you identify everything that seems toxic to you or negative, or that gets in the way of your relationship with others, the way you organize your life or your environment. Like Camille, you can write a list of "I no longer want . . ." *Cleaning outside means* looking at your lifestyle to see how it can be improved, from getting rid of useless or damaged things to sorting your possessions out and throwing away what you don't want or need, tidying, redecorating . . .

Moments of Gratitude: Each day, think about everything that has been positive, from the least significant to the most (a delicious early-morning cup of coffee; the great joy of a personal triumph), and say "thank you."

Positive Anchoring: This is a technique that will put you in a receptive mood—in other words, in a favorable physical and mental state. How? By reactivating the sensations you felt at a happy moment in your life. To do this you need to create an anchor: in a calm place, visualize the happy moment you wish to recall, and associate it with a word, image, or gesture. With training, you will be able to recover the anchor by reproducing the gesture or word, or by recalling the associated image, and thus rediscover the desired emotional state.

Positive Notebook: This is a book in which you note down, in alphabetical order, your successes and joys, both large and small. How? For each letter of the alphabet, think of keywords that suggest significant, positive moments. For example: A for Adrien (the happy times spent with your child); L for Love (your most beautiful romantic moments); M for Marbella (somewhere that reminds you of a memorable holiday) or Martial Arts (perhaps you won a medal and remembering it makes you proud). Describe your memory as precisely as possible—the surroundings, the people involved—and also outline your physical and emotional response.

Positive Thoughts and Attitude: Your words give off vibes. So does your physical attitude. Both of them greatly influence your mind-set and therefore your reality. That is why it is good to adopt positive thoughts and posture. Stand upright rather than hunched, smile rather than scowl, see the positive in everything instead of complaining and becoming discouraged. Train yourself to look on the bright side; when you speak, make it sound positive and not negative, use the active form of verbs rather than the passive. To say "I'll never do it in time" is not the same as saying "I face up to difficulties by getting organized and mobilizing my resources." It's up to you!

Power Songs: Download a playlist of music that makes you feel as if you have wings.

Promises Notebook: This notebook is for you to write down the objectives you have set for yourself and the promises you have made to yourself, to help you remain fully committed to your resolutions. And make sure you tick off each one as it is accomplished. Remember that the most important thing is not to know what needs to be done but to do it. Just do it!

Red Card: This is a small signal you can agree on with your partner (or child) to warn them that an argument is brewing. It is like a red warning light in a car. This can help avoid aggression taking hold.

Reproach Machine Gun: This is the weapon we use when we start our sentences with a "you" of reproach ("You never think about . . ."; "You plonk yourself in front of your computer without asking me if . . ."). This is strictly forbidden, because it always ends with us caught up in a spiral of aggression. Better to learn to express your grievances with an "I."

SMART Method: This will help you define the goals you wish to achieve and give you the greatest chance of achieving them. You need to ensure that your objective is Specific (clearly defined and adapted), Measurable (so you can assess when the goal is achieved), Attainable (defined in a realistic way, divided into a series of accessible goals; it should not be the "unreachable star"), Realistic (in order to stay motivated, your objective should match your capabilities), and Timely (you need to set yourself a deadline).

Steam Off Stamps: This means that you dare to say what is troubling you and you express your feelings as soon as there is any unease or conflict, whether this is latent or not. This will help you avoid any pressure-cooker explosions.

Swear-Jar: This is your anti-wallowing kitty! Make your swear-jar out of a jam jar or similar. The idea is that each time you catch yourself wallowing in negative thoughts, you put money in the jar. The whole family can join in!

Theory of Small Steps: This theory tells us that it is advisable to see the process of change as a series of small steps, small transformations, rather than an enormous mountain that has to be scaled in one go. This makes it seem less daunting, and the result will be even more rewarding.

Acknowledgments

A huge thanks to Stéphanie Ricordel and Élodie Dusseaux, my editors at Eyrolles, for having believed in my project and allowing it to see the light of day.

An equally big thanks to Stéphanie, my twin sister, and to my mother. They have both helped and supported me with their kind and constructive advice throughout the writing of the book.

Thanks finally to my son, Vadim, for being what he is and for bringing me so much happiness.

Your Second Life Begins When You Realize You Only Have One

RAPHAËLLE GIORDANO

Discussion Guide

———

A Conversation
with Raphaëlle Giordano

PUTNAM
— EST. 1838 —

Discussion Guide

• • •

1. Why do you think Camille feels as if her life is missing something at the beginning of the novel? Do you relate to her character? Why or why not?

2. Why does Camille decide to go with Claude's unorthodox therapy? Would you have called him? Why or why not?

3. Have you ever had a case of "routinitis?" What helped you to climb out of your rut? What strategies from the novel would you try in your own life?

4. On p. 11, Claude says "The capacity for being happy has to be worked on, built up day by day." Do you agree with him? How do you think you could start building this capacity in your own life?

5. Claude teaches Camille the "theory of small steps" (p. 29), asking her to start by listing out everything she'd like to change in her life. What are the top three things you want to change in your own life?

6. Claude reminds Camille that "many people know what they're supposed to do to lead a happy life but never really put it into practice" (p. 70). Do you think that's true? What do you think might be holding people back?

7. What would you say are your top three successes in your life? Why do you think these three achievements mean so much to you? What could you do to create similar success in the next year of your life?

8. What do you think about Claude's "elastic band" theory? Have you seen this play out in your own life?

9. Do you have a role model? If so, who is it? What is it you admire about them? What is one thing you could do tomorrow to emulate these qualities?

10. Think back on the past few days in your life. What things would you list in your Positive Notebook?

11. Claude teaches Camille to "anchor" herself in a positive memory. Have you ever tried this exercise before? How do

you think it might change your perspective? What anchor would you choose for yourself?

12. Were you surprised by the novel's ending?

*A Conversation
with Raphaëlle Giordano*

• • •

What inspired you to write this novel?

I've been carrying Camille's story with me for a long time. The book isn't autobiographical, but just like Camille, I also experienced an important turning point in my life. Specifically, right after my experience working as the creative director of a communications agency in Paris, where I was having a rather difficult time. That experience drove me to leave the business world and put myself first. I decided to take the road less traveled and to throw myself into a much more artistic lifestyle. Though it was less stable, it felt like it fit who I was and my most important life aspirations. Over the past ten to fifteen years, I've done a lot of searching and reflecting about who I was, who I am, and who I want to be in my life. I've experimented and thought a lot about different techniques people can use to go about achieving their wildest dreams. It takes a lot of creativity. My life experience made it easy for me to write Camille's story, because I understand the twists and turns that happen on the road to transformation.

While *Your Second Life Begins When You Realize You Only Have One* is your first novel, you've published nonfiction books before. What was different about writing fiction?
Writing fiction feels much more fluid than writing nonfiction. I used to be a graphic designer, so I'm a very visual person. So, when I write this type of story, I have to use metaphors and I have to make my writing really visual. That's what feels natural to me.

The title *Your Second Life Begins When You Realize You Only Have One* is so fun! How did you come up with it?
In a lot of the creative fields, you do group brainstorming. It was actually my son's father who came up with the title after some brainstorming and internet searches. Both of us used to work in publicity in creative fields, so we're trained to come up with titles, slogans, and catchy phrases. We find these phrases through word associations—doing what I call a "creative sweep." You just let your brain go in every possible direction and try to find something interesting. He came up with the title while searching for themes related to happiness, this moment where we really start living. He found a quote from Confucius that fit the book perfectly but was a little too long. Once I had the quote, the hard part was modifying and shortening it.

Camille is an utterly charming and relatable narrator. Is she inspired by anyone you know? How much do you have in common with her?

Camille was a spokeswoman for my ideas. It's funny—I'm Camille, but I'm also Claude, and I switch between the two. Both characters helped me deliver the messages that I wanted to get across to my readers. I do have a lot in common with Camille, and so do other people I know. I've had periods in my life when I suffered from "routinitis"—when I felt like I needed to be living a deeper and fuller romantic and professional life. Many of us have a lot in common with Camille, myself especially, having a path that wasn't totally straightforward. We have more than one life to live within the life we are given. It's rare in this day and age to continue doing the same thing for your entire life. We have to ask ourselves questions when we have "Camille moments." I've definitely felt the way she does in the book. I left a professional situation that wasn't working for me. I reinvented my life. I started living the life that I wanted to live. I started writing books and, though it felt risky, I stuck with it, and it worked out.

How did you come up with the diagnosis of "routinitis?" Have you ever had a case of routinitis?

It's true that I invented the word; it doesn't actually exist. Making up words is something I learned to do when I worked in publicity. To answer the second part of the question, I have definitely gone through periods when I felt like I wasn't achieving my potential or my dreams. It was awful. I hung on and did a lot of reflection. Then I spent years creating the life I have now. I wanted to share what I learned from that process with my readers, share what really helped me get on this path. The book isn't just me babbling, this is what, in my experience, actually worked to escape an unfulfilling life and start living a life of meaning.

In your past, you ran a company that organizes events focused on stress management, team and relationship building, and finding creativity. How did you decide to do this work? How did this job and your background influence your novel?

When I decided to leave the stability of my job at the communications agency, I knew I had to find a new job that would be interesting, but also would give me the time and space to reawaken my artistic side—whether that was painting or writing. I needed a job that would give me time to create, follow my path, and figure out if I could actually pursue an artistic career. The stars aligned, as they sometimes do, leading me to discover this amazing career as a creative events planner—facilitating group teambuilding activities, making people work together creatively to strengthen motivation and creative potential, for example: forming connections among people by having them work together on a giant painted piece. It was perfect, because the work was fulfilling, but I sometimes didn't work more than three or four days per month. The rest of the time I could work on my first books, which was where my real passion lay. So, how did that job influence the book? It allowed me to experiment and to prove that anything is possible. It's just a question of organization, of creating structures that will help you achieve your dreams. You just have to come up with some methods, and then, little by little, you can build a dream. So, I want my success today to be a testimony to perseverance, daring, and hard work. There is no magic spell, but hard work pays off and it is possible to turn your dreams into reality.

Claude teaches Camille many useful tricks for finding happiness and improving her life. How did you come up with these strategies? Are they strategies you've been taught or did you invent any of them?

Claude's advice is a mixture of advice I've heard and strategies I discovered when I was going through a difficult time about fourteen years ago. I really needed to reinvent my life. So, yes, Claude's advice is based on existing techniques, but I adapted most of the real exercises somewhat, and then others I just made up, because that was the nature of my job—to mix the creative and the visual, like the imaginary camera, the positivity journal, and the goals folder. There are other true influences that show just beneath the surface: emotional intelligence and personality type, such as Process Communication or MBTI (Myers Briggs Type Indicator), in which I'm certified, transactional analysis, etc. Overall, I made up all of the events in the book, but I drew upon my true experiences. Parts of Claude are also based on my real-life "routinologist" my mother, whose name is Claude (Claude is both a man's and a woman's name).

Do you have a favorite challenge that Camille faces? Are you currently practicing any of her stages in your own life? Is there one challenge that you find hardest to enact for yourself?

All of Camille's challenges are interesting. One that I like to do regularly is "Operation Blank Space." It always does me so much good. You clean up your space and your mind at the same time. It's so helpful to surround yourself with beauty and make your environment into an inspiring place. I find that doing this regularly has really positive results. What's the most challenging, though it seems crazy, is letting yourself slow down—taking the time to relax. The more we have on our plates, the more important it is that we prioritize relaxation. Yes, it can be hard to make this relaxation happen, but especially when we're feeling overwhelmed by everything we have to do, we have to remember to pause. I always try to keep that in mind. Time spent relaxing, doing nothing, simply pausing, is never wasted time. We don't lose time, but we gain reality. It's extremely powerful.

You're also known as an artist and a painter. Why do you think creativity is important? What's the first piece of advice you have for someone looking to bring more creativity into their own life?

Creativity is one of the most amazing aspects of our existence. It's a state when we are free and connected to the child within us. It's a state, an energy, of spontaneity and joie de vivre. I often try to access this state in my life. Honestly, it helps me time and time again in personal and professional situations. Creativity opens up the maximum amount of possibilities. When we feel like we are stuck in a box, creativity can help us find a way out, and there is always a way out. To develop your creativity, there are thousands of little things that you can do in your everyday life. You just have to train yourself. You should open up your spirit and always stay curious. You can keep a notebook and write about what you see, movies, art, plays—all the things that nourish your creativity. Training yourself to be creative means breaking out of your routines, taking new paths, and trying things for the first time. Creativity is like a muscle and over time, it will get stronger. We have to let go of our desire to always be perfect and to control everything. This stretches our minds and souls and gives us more and more access to that creative state.

You live in Paris, France, but it's clear the novel has hit a nerve with readers all over the world. Why do you think Camille's story is so universally important?

I think Camille's story is relevant to so many people because we all carry our childhood dreams with us, but sometimes we feel like we will never achieve them, and that can be heartbreaking. I think we all have a desire to make our lives as beautiful and impressive as they can be. So many people are caught in a kind of rat race and they don't take the time to think—who am I? What is the meaning of my existence? We place so much value on material things, but if that is all we are working for, it becomes demoralizing, an existential crisis. It's so important to take the time to find ourselves. Why? Because what gives life meaning, as Socrates said, is knowing oneself. We have to look inside ourselves to know who we really are, because that's what will help us find ways of spending time that will allow us to give the best versions of ourselves to the world. We have to create our own definitions of success and happiness. You can't use your neighbor's definition. It is not egotistical to think this way. When we have the best possible energy, we can contribute the most beautiful parts of ourselves to the world, and that's an admirable goal. The idea of success is so subjective. It has nothing to do with who makes the most money or who has the most impressive career. Some of the greatest heroes are seemingly ordinary people who really touch the lives of others—people in need, people who they are close to, their children. That's what's important. To have goals that are less material and more spiritual. That's what really counts as a beautiful life, a life full of achievements, a life full of happiness.

RAPHAËLLE GIORDANO is a writer, personal development expert, artist, and certified psychologist. Before starting her own events agency specializing in artistic programming, she studied at the École Supérieure Estienne for Applied Arts and worked at several communications agencies in Paris. *Your Second Life Begins When You Realize You Only Have One* is Giordano's first novel. She lives in Paris, France.

VISIT RAPHAËLLE GIORDANO ONLINE

raphaellegiordano.com